THE ROSWELL CONSPIRACY

Chapter One:
"Dark Days"

a novel

by

J.A.R. Darrell and John Darin

iUniverse, Inc.
New York Bloomington

The Roswell Conspiracy

Copyright © 2008 by J.A.R. Darrell and John Darin

All rights reserved. No part of this book may be used or reproduced by any means, graphic, electronic, or mechanical, including photocopying, recording, taping or by any information storage retrieval system without the written permission of the publisher except in the case of brief quotations embodied in critical articles and reviews.

This is a work of fiction. All of the characters, names, incidents, organizations, and dialogue in this novel are either the products of the author's imagination or are used fictitiously.

iUniverse books may be ordered through booksellers or by contacting:

iUniverse
1663 Liberty Drive
Bloomington, IN 47403
www.iuniverse.com
1-800-Authors (1-800-288-4677)

Because of the dynamic nature of the Internet, any Web addresses or links contained in this book may have changed since publication and may no longer be valid. The views expressed in this work are solely those of the author and do not necessarily reflect the views of the publisher, and the publisher hereby disclaims any responsibility for them.

ISBN: 978-0-595-48369-3 (pbk)
ISBN: 978-0-595-60460-9 (cloth)
ISBN: 978-0-595-51500-4 (ebk)

Printed in the United States of America

Cover design by Linda Manion

THE AMERICAN CLARION

Compiled from various eye witness accounts

For a number of reasons beyond this newspaper's control, reasons now obvious to even the most casual reader of these pages, the following report is highly unusual.

Certainly the most remarkable aspect remains the total lack of electronic communications between our local newsroom and the far-flung news bureaus that regularly furnish our source reports from all over the globe.

Normally, our practice for any story would require that we verify all pertinent details through at least three independent sources. You will no doubt understand, given the extraordinary circumstances described in the preceding paragraph, why that is not possible in this case.

What we do know is this. All electrical power, all broadcast operations, internet, radar, electric lighting, all forms of modern high-tech society, have fallen dark.

Our sense of the affected area's size is limited to those distances our correspondents have been able to travel on foot or horseback or by other means of non-mechanized transport. Even so, the dark zone does bear all the appearance of being quite large and the technology blackout in all cases, total.

In fact, most notably to our own enterprise, this report you are now reading is being set by hand, using movable type borrowed from Miller-Christian University's historical wing, a technique more suitable to an era nearly a century past, perhaps even as far back as to the days of Benjamin Franklin.

After it is typed on a mechanical typewriter and edited, this story will be printed using two crank-operated hand presses on loan from the same university, then distributed by bicycle messengers specially hired by this newspaper.

To Albert Enstein, Carl Sagen and all the visionaries who saw beyond our limits into the Universe ... and the future.

Acknowledgements

The authors wish to acknowledge the following for their influencee and support of the concept of a Roswell Conspiracy.

The Roswell Museum and Research Center, Roswell, New Mexico, and its director, Dennis G. Balthaser.

Colonel Philip J. Corso, author of "The Day After Roswell"

Steven Speilberg and George Lucas for their films, "Star Wars:, "Close Encounters of the Third Kind", "E.T.", and the "Indiana Jones" series.

The producers of "The Day the Earth Stood Still"

The producers of "Independence Day"

The producers of "Contact"

And the countless other films, books and stories regarding the Roswell Incident and the possibility of alien contact with our world.

... prologue

Rolling black cubes through an inhospitable darkness that spread the stars in Orion's Arm. Dice sans pips, with no fair way to reckon the score, winner or loser, strangers take all.

Blue world full of chatter and click, secrets and power bought on the move, used on the fly.

Most below knew nothing.

Two knew it all.

... part one

"It has become appallingly obvious that our technology has exceeded our humanity."
Albert Einstein

Chapter I
"City Lights"

A labored breathing -- more than the common movement of air across a mostly-flat landscape -- disturbed the boughs and ruffled the fall foliage, wind-chime crisp and colorless in the early-morning gray.

Something out there in the blur between day and night screeched, feline and wild. It was a hunter's voice, accompanied by a stealthy, here-and-there rustling through the underbrush.

In whatever cause the general agitation came, it carried with it a disturbing smell, not exactly the tangy, ozone stab of singed oxygen. More, it seemed, what might possibly be - lacking an objective point of reference – the genuine stench of brimstone.

That thought alone might have caused unease –had anyone seen, heard, tasted it – not true terror, perhaps, but at least unease.

But not one of those senses came into play from such an external, omnipotent place of vantage. No one lurked there in the darkness to listen, watch and sniff the roiled night.

And, in unaltered fact, all else lay most peacefully at perfect rest. The familiarity of the moon, bloated this night to a full harvest roundness and sunken low, held itself in place, laced to the dark sky by occasional lights, trailing long, bright stitchings, that crossed and crisscrossed above a two-story frame house, tall tree shadows gathered around it, that clung to a rather ordinary hill top.

A dark window in the house, one on the ground level, began to glow faintly. A smaller firefly light drifted away from the first, soon vanished briefly to reappear on the floor just above, past one glass pane, another. A door opened into a third room. The light shone brighter.

"Last warning, Caleb."

Sara Burwell, eighteen, slender, pretty even in her floor-length gray dress, could by nature, turn bossy at times. And whenever she did, if heard from another room, she sounded enough like her mother to fool even a son's ear.

As if eliminating any hope of escape, she had positioned herself in the room's only doorway, holding a kerosene lamp just above her shoulder level so that its light spilled into the room, reflected off a mirror above a dresser, and made stark shadows around the Spartan furnishings, especially the bed, where a lone figure lay unmoved by her abrupt arrival, especially the intrusion of the light she brought with her.

Sara sighed heavily, pushed herself forward, seemed almost to float across the threshold to the bedside, where she bent lithely and whipped back the covers to expose her twin brother, Caleb, clad in long johns, lying with his back to her.

"Breakfast's on the table."

Caleb rolled over, surprised. He wore bright yellow buds plugged into his ears that emitted heavy-metal music when he pulled them away from his head.

"If Pa catches you with that, there'll be the devil to pay. He wants you down in the kitchen right now."

Caleb smirked at her.

"Who, Pa or the devil?"

Without waiting for the scolding that her face told him she was about to give him, he quickly hid the earphones and a small radio under the mattress and set the bare soles of his feet on the floor. He quickly withdrew them again and pulled on a pair of heavy socks.

Sara turned away.

He whispered after her, "Don't tell, okay?"

She glared back, watched him stand up, "Have I ever?'

"No."

"Hurry then."

As she carried all the light with her out of the room, the clatter of dishes and metal utensils drifted up from below to fill the empty space she left behind her.

Caleb hurriedly pulled on a pair of trousers, his boots and a plain shirt and half ran out into a short hallway and down the stairs to the ground floor, where a left turn took him out of the front mud room and into the kitchen, where his father, Seth, locked his dark eyes with Caleb's and watched him enter, still pulling his suspenders up over his shoulders.

Caleb slid into a chair at the far end of the table from Seth.

"Nice of you to join us, Caleb."

"Yes sir."

"Any danger, by your own estimation of such matters, that you might end up actually sleeping through Judgment Day?"

"Hope not, Pa."

"Uh-huh."

Miriam Burwell, wife and mother, turned from the wood-burning stove and smiled at Caleb.

"Morning, Son."

"Ma."

Halfway through her thirties, Miriam wore her hair pulled severely back from her face in a fashion that, while likely to lessen the beauty of any other woman, only emphasized her own.

She brought coffee and filled Seth's cup.

He caught her hand and kissed it.

"I'm a lucky man."

She smiled.

"Being as how a righteous wife never argues with her husband, I suppose I must agree with your assessment of me."

She leaned down and whispered in his ear, "The boy's still growing, Husband. It might not hurt to let him sleep a bit more than you and I might need."

"Hmmm ..."

Seth watched as Miriam set food in front of Caleb and touched his cheek.

Without answering, Caleb lowered his head, and the room fell respectfully silent as he clasped his hands under his chin, thanked God for the food he would soon eat and other blessings. The others had no way of knowing that he also begged for the strength to bear up under his father's frequent rebukes. He whispered, "Amen," opened his eyes and took up the fork beside his plate.

"Your mother spoils you, Caleb."

Caleb swallowed a mouthful of food that seemed to go down hard.

"I'm sorry I disappoint you so much, Pa."

Seth's eyes meet Miriam's; and they softened a bit. "But in as much as my own father used to say much the same thing about me, I suppose it must be part of a mother's job description."

He pushed his chair back, stood and looked down the table at Caleb.

"Try not to take all morning."

At the door, he pulled on a heavy coat and hat and without looking back, went outside.

As the door shut, Caleb laid down his fork and rested his forehead in both hands.

"Could somebody please say why he hates me so much?"

Miriam brought her hand up to her mouth.

"Oh, Caleb."

But Sara was having none of it. "Don't be foolish."

"Then what makes him be that way?"

"Might be Pa'd treat you more like a man, if you once in a while acted like one," Sara suggested to him.

Miriam waved her daughter away. "Hush, Sara." Then she turned to look at Caleb. "Your father's worried you're so drawn to the outside world, son."

Caleb brought another bite to his mouth. He sighed. "And he pretends it isn't there."

Sara stood up and walked off a few paces. "Pa knows, Caleb, that you'll leave here, first chance you get."

"Yeah, and it'll be mostly because of him, too."

"Stop! Just stop it, now!" As Miriam wiped her eyes on her apron, the air in the room grew very thick. She straightened her already neat hair. "He'll have the team hitched by now."

Caleb took a couple more bites, then stood, went to the coat rack and dressed for the outdoors.

"Another exciting day moving hay from over here to over there." He struck a match and lit the wick in a lantern. "Don't know how we ever stand the pace."

He turned his back on them then and, going outside, shut the door hard behind him.

Ø

Caleb descended the front steps into a farmyard lit only by his lantern and what little light spilled out of the kitchen windows.

A flatbed wagon, driven by Seth and drawn by two huge horses, rattled to a stop just beyond the white washed gate. And as Caleb climbed up beside Seth, he paused to look at the sky, where the light streaks laced east and west, north and south with ever-greater frequency.

Seth glanced up, too.

"That's none of our business, son. We've got some hay to move."

Caleb settled himself beside his father. "Yes sir."

"Hyaaa!" yelled Seth in concert with a snap of the reins in his practiced hands.

As the wagon jerked forward, the frigid peace of the farm, faintly reddened by the first slice of sunlight, moved in close about them and embraced them. There was something vexing about that nudging and nagging from some peripheral corner of Caleb's mind.

"Pa, doesn't it seem like it might be darker than usual?" He pointed toward the near horizon. "I can't see any light coming from town."

Seth looked and pulled in the reins. "Whoa."

The wagon stopped.

Seth scanned the eastern sky beyond the end of their road. "You're right. It's always bright over there, day or night."

One of the horses snorted in an equine way mostly reserved for occasions of extreme anxiety. Both animals fidgeted in their harnesses and stamped the ground; one came up a little ways off his front hooves.

"Easy." Seth soothed them with other soft sounds that were almost words. Then he slid back into human speech.

"Probably just spooked by that wild cat -- with his radio collar -- strayed off the preserve again."

Caleb wrinkled his nose.

"Pa."

"Yes, I smell it, too."

The horses continued to wheeze nervously.

"I don't hear any cars on the highway either, Pa."

Seth nodded and said, "Something's sure not right. We might should get back to the house right now."

"Look!" Caleb pointed back the way they had just come, toward their home, where one of the flying lights zipped low over the roof, taking a lightning rod with it, passed with a hiss through the tree tops, and whistled over a low rise, where it obviously came to ground without the slightest sound or other proof of impact.

The horses screamed in unison. The white leaped forward and to the left, the black to the right and they ran.

"Lord help us," breathed Seth.

He and Caleb fell back onto the wagon seat, with Seth calling out, "Whoa! Whoa!" all to no avail.

The wagon bounced high, nearly flipped over, its wheels striking a rut, the whole thing lurching hard to one side.

"Jump, Caleb; get yourself clear!"

"Pa!"

"Now, Caleb!"

They leaped. The horses and wagon careened off into the darkness.

Chapter 2
"Dark Motives"

"Get away!" Tiffany Diamond screamed down from the roof of the TV news van. Beside her, Ricky Escobar, a state-of-the-art video camera tucked under his arm, kicked at one of the figures who was trying to scale up the vehicle's side.

The fellow moaned and fell back into the warp and woof of a grumbling darkness so profoundly heavy that it offered no real sense of the city's great size or the depths of its grand architectural canyons.

All the worse, it gave comfort and concealment to those who brought with them into the chaos their own dark motives.

"Hey gorgeous," a faceless shadow yelled up from the crowd that by then was making a sport of rocking the van. "How 'bout you come down here so I can protect you from these scumbags?"

Tiffany had covered her share of dangerous stories, but death had never before reached out for her from such an intimate nearness.

Nor was there comfort whenever one of the damnable lights sizzled overhead, threw its greenish glow earthward over the broad avenue where the van sat, and showed them the dark high-rise facades and dead cars and knots of milling humanity.

It was only in those intervals that the overwhelming magnitude of the unfolding disaster could fully reveal itself.

Another streak of fire went by. And some fool actually shot up at it with a handgun of a patently worthless caliber.

Worse yet, as Tiffany reflexively ducked away from the gunfire, her shoe sole slipped on the metal car roof. She screamed as she skidded toward the edge.

"Ricky!"

He caught her by one arm and dragged her back up beside him.

"Aw, c'mon," yelled one of the figures below. He leaped up and made a determined grab for her ankle.

Ricky swung the camera, hit the man hard.

"Pig!" he screamed; and the man flipped backward into the mob.

There came quite soon after that the piercing shrill of whistles, at least a pair of them; and two uniformed policemen waded into the crowd, their nightsticks flailing the air in the light of another overhead flash. Hard wood whacked dully against retreating flesh, forming a sickening staccato.

But in fact the swirl of violence quickly flowed outward, away from the van, forced along by one of the officers.

"Here ma'am," said the other cop, as he held up a blood-spattered glove to Tiffany. "They're all gone. It's safe to come down now."

She and Ricky scrambled down to the pavement.

"Thank God you got here when you did."

The cop immediately recognized her.

"Hey, you're Tiffany Diamond, the TV reporter."

"Yes, more than a little worse for the wear, I fear."

"Human nature, ma'am. Scared people just doing whatever they can to hide how scared they really are."

The other cop came back out of the surrounding darkness.

"You guys really shouldn't ought to be out here."

"We're trying to get to my father's apartment," Tiffany told them. "It's just around the corner."

"C'mon then, we'll take you there while we still can."

As they started off together, Ricky examined his camera by the light of the occasional small fire. "Damn ... it's busted."

Tiffany locked her arm through his.

"Be glad that's all that's broken, babe."

But he continued poking at the camera.

"Andy'll have my butt if I don't get this."

"I really doubt if Andy's giving much thought to your skinny little butt right now."

Chapter 3
"What's a Quigley?"

Tiffany and Ricky, accompanied by the two police officers rounded a corner some distance from where they had left the news van. They approached an ornate door beneath a canopy signed Morton Arms.

A sleek, black sedan of unfamiliar manufacture and most curious design sat at the curb.

At their approach, a fellow in a doorman's uniform struck a cigarette lighter and held it up. "Hell of a morning, ain't it, Miss Diamond?"

"It sure is, Arnie. Is my father home?"

"Yes ma'am. But I'm afraid the lift's out."

They all three went inside the front door, where Arnie pointed to a table.

"There's candles and matches there. Help yourself."

"Thanks. Are you okay?"

He shrugged and said, "I'm worried about my family."

"You should leave. Go home to them, now."

"I dunno."

Tiffany lit a candle. "They come first."

"Yes, ma'am."

Ø

Tiffany and Ricky's labored breathing echoed up and down the stairwell.

They had been following the flickering glow of their candles, shielding the flames with cupped hands.

As Ricky passed a sign reading: "12TH FLOOR", he stopped and looked up. "Your father had to live in the penthouse, right?"

"Never hurts to have friends in high places." Tiffany grinned as she passed him. "You're just out of shape is all. There it is."

She opened a door labeled "Penthouse", which led out of the stairwell and into a broad hallway, where they paused to steady their breathing.

"Twelve flights," gasped Ricky. "Twelve flights, me lugging a camera and audio crap."

"Whining does not become a grown man, Ricky. C'mon."

They crossed to a pair of wooden doors, where Tiffany knocked hard.

"Daddy."

Immediately one of the doors opened to frame Dan Diamond, debonair and composed, and despite the prevailing circumstances, immaculately dressed in a suit and tie. He held a sputtering storm lamp.

"Tiffany, I was worried sick."

Tiffany hugged Dan's neck. "Daddy, this is Ricky, my cameraman."

"Hi Ricky. It's good you were with her when this happened. Both of you, get yourselves inside here."

Tiffany and Ricky moved through the doorway and entered a candlelit space that offered an atmosphere of tasteful wealth. Dan ushered the two of them into the living room.

In Dan's presence, Tiffany's voice became almost childlike. "What's going on, Daddy?"

But it was not her father's voice that answered her. The words, in a silky and cultured baritone with the faint hint of a London accent, came from somewhere else in the room. It said, "All light is gone from the world, Madam. That is what has happened."

They all turned, Tiffany and Ricky surprised, Dan smiling thinly as a smallish yet well-proportioned man of unidentifiable age or nationality stepped from shadows near a bookcase. He wore a three-piece suit with a gold chain draped across the vest front. "And I am afraid it has abandoned us all to mortal danger."

Ø

In the silence that followed the unexpected appearance of the man in the three-piece suit, Dan cleared his throat.

"This is Mister Quigley. He and I were about to take a little trip."

Quigley opened the ornate outer case of a gold watch attached to the other end of the chain. The timepiece just seemed to have jumped from his vest pocket and into his hand the instant he need it.

Addressing just Dan alone Quigley said, "It's time, sir."

Tiffany, always the reporter, eyed the extraordinary little man with unveiled suspicion. "A trip to where?"

"Well –", Dan started to say.

Quigley quickly interrupted, "One can only say, to a place of refuge." The voice by that time had achieved basso profundo, leaving Dan's own sounding a trifle thinner than usual.

"Yes. And, by our good luck, now you two can go with us."

Quigley swiveled on the balls of his feet and mildly rebuked Dan with his unblinking eyes.

"No sir. I regret to say that such a alteration to the plan would not be a part of my instructions."

"Well, if you think I'm leaving Tiffany here in this mess, you are most sadly mistaken."

"Oh dear, Mister Diamond –"

Tiffany crossed to where Quigley stood; and she marched a short half circle in front of him as she said, "And I'm not going anywhere without Ricky."

Quigley shrugged at Dan. "There, you see?"

Dan glanced at the darkness beyond the window along one entire side of his living room.

"Your words give me cause to wonder, Mister Quigley, just how serious your employer really is about seeing me."

"Very serious, I assure you, Mister Diamond."

"Then I guess that's that," Dan told him, as he turned toward Tiffany and Ricky. "We go as we are, sans baggage."

He started for the door. But Ricky held his ground.

"My camera."

Dan looked back. "Yes … that might be important. Bring it."

When Quigley hesitated, Dan smiled charmingly.

"Are we ready, Quigley?"

Quigley nodded, a bit miffed, and followed them toward the door.

"We are ready, sir, with all else to be sorted out once we reach our destination."

He rushed past the others and they followed him out the door.

Chapter 4
"Exit Strategy"

By the time they had descended to the building's lobby, matters in the street outside had already deteriorated to something resembling a state of genuine anarchy.

Arnie the doorman was nowhere to be seen, apparently having taken Tiffany's advice and abandoned his post in favor of seeing to his family's safety.

One of the glass doors leading in off the sidewalk had obviously suffered some sort of attack, with a crack that ran most of the way from floor to ceiling; though it had not shattered out of its frame.

Quigley paused before opening the door with the key left stuck in the lock, probably by Arnie.

"We wait just another moment or perhaps two, while the hooligans migrate to the next block," Quigley whispered loudly enough for them all to hear him quite clearly. "I think now is as safe as it will be."

He turned the lock and after they had all stepped outside, he relocked the door and dropped the key in through the mail slot.

"Quickly now."

They moved on muffled footfalls into a night lit only by the odd trash fire; and, unmolested, they slipped inside the black car parked out front.

Quigley took the wheel.

The little man pressed a dashboard button, which seemed responsible for the faint whoosh under the hood. And second later, they were on their way.

Tiffany leaned forward from a rear seat.

"How is it that this car works, when all the others don't."

Without looking from the way ahead, Quigley replied, "My employer is an eccentric man who trusts in old-fashioned things, like steam powered vehicles heated with propane."

"At least I can believe the eccentric part," Tiffany agreed. She looked at her father. "Where are we going?"

Dan hesitated. "Can I say the state, Mister Quigley?"

"Only that," came Quigley's voice crisply.

Dan studied his daughter in the near darkness. "We're bound for Maryland, Tiffany. And that's about all I know myself."

Tiffany mouthed the word back at him as a question.

"Maryland?"

She and Ricky looked at one another and shrugged.

Chapter 5
"Sun Rise"

The sun made an uneasy approach on the city, slowly shortening the shadows that hung like funerary bunting down the long building faces.

In its coming, the light brought with it nothing so remote as comfort. Not seeing had been a better choice than having the immediacy of the horror revealed in all its remarkable savagery.

From pools of residual gloom, beyond where the car's acetylene head lamps sweep clear their way, they saw hunched shadows hauling things of bulk and weight from various shops. More than once, they spied human figures, in various postures of discard, silent and unmoving forms on the sidewalks, in the gutters and in the streets.

Gangs roamed everywhere and seemed to compete with one another in their acts of wanton brutality.

Repeatedly the mobs charged the car, banging its windows with sticks and pipes.

Only Quigley remained calm inside.

The others cringed and clung to one another in terror. Amazingly, the glass and the metal managed to hold itself together.

In every block, police officers used traffic flares to light crime scenes of escalating savagery.

And there were, without ending, the screams. They filled the darkness and multiplied with the approach of day. And like the gunshots, they arrived from every side to fill that final ebb of night.

And just as dawn pinked the eastern sky, Quigley drove the black car out of the last of the exburbs; and they rolled into the calm of a just-stirring countryside.

The journey was not over.

It had barely begun.

Chapter 6
Coffee, Tea or Answers?

Finally, exhausted, Tiffany dozed briefly, coming awake surprised to find she had slept at all. She was astonished, too, that they had left the main highway.

She had, she guessed, been jostled up from slumber by the rutted back road that carried the car and all of them with it, through winding stands of old-growth trees that lined both sides of their way.

The gnarled trunks, she reasoned, must support a canopy of leaves and branches thick enough to hold back the sun and to hide them from airborne observers, if there were any such things still around.

She could not know that that particular question would soon find an answer.

In the meantime, another had just occurred to her. She leaned forward across the front seat back and asked of Quigley, "How far have we come?"

"We are part-way to our destination," he replied with vexing ambiguity, even as they came out of the trees and squinted at a sudden sliver of sunlight that lit a large metal building beside a broad gravel strip.

Quigley stopped the car in the shadow of the building and they all crawled out to begin the process of re-circulating blood into their legs.

Quigley selected Ricky. "Would you please give me a hand opening the doors?"

They pushed; and as the two halves grated in opposing directions, a bit of dim morning's light leaked inside and fell across a curious craft with long, wide wings and a translucent airframe.

Tiffany's jaw dropped. "We're going to fly in that?"

Without a pause, Quigley smiled thinly and for only the first time; and he said, "I promise you, it's really quite safe."

He opened a hatchway in the plane's flank and dragged out two cranks, one of which he pressed into Dan's uncertain hands.

"Everyone works, Mister Diamond. So, if you'll insert that end into the slot just there in the cowling; and when I tell you, turn it clockwise."

As Dan followed the instructions, Quigley took the other crank, jammed it into a second opposing opening, and quite simply said, "Now."

He and Dan twisted with the two cranks, clockwise on one side of the cowling, counter-clockwise on the other.

To the others Quigley smugly confided, "We are storing kinetic energy in the fly wheels that feed torque to the propellers."

And quite soon, as a faint whine filled the hanger, Quigley removed his crank. "Everybody inside."

He hopped into the pilot's seat. The others clambered in behind him.

And with its high-tech propellers whispering a confident hum, the peculiar craft rolled free of the hanger and bumped along over the run-up to the gravel strip.

In an officious voice unexpectedly tinged with humor, Quigley said, "I know when you travel you have many choices for airlines. I'd like to thank you for flying Air Quigley."

Then as dawn broke fully clear of the horizon, the plane made a dash down the runway, rotated its nose skyward, and lifted effortlessly into the air.

Chapter 7
"A Reward, Maybe?"

A hot wind caught sand off the desert floor near the mesa and lifted it into a tiny vortex that made from that point a drunken confusion of is progress into a dry arroyo. It melted there in the varicose creek bed and rejoined the common firmament without a trace.

Overhead, across a cloudless sky, a single fleet dot made apparent play of swooping and diving. A high-pitched whistle cut the whispering air. And a man's voice called out, "Iye!"

Two riders on horseback came on slowly through rippling heat rising off the rocky, dry deserted earth.

Kimama Sweet, comfortable in the saddle, a face of sculpted beauty, tanned skin and shiny black hair that hung long across her shoulders, stopped her mount in a saguaro's thin shade.

"He's ignoring you," she said to her male companion, Akando Kenyon, youthful and lithe of form, easily mounted, teeth revealed white between smiling lips.

"Iye does not ignore me," he laughed as he reined in beside Kimama. "Here he comes now."

Surely enough, just as he extended his right arm, a fiercely magnificent falcon settled onto it, gaining its balance just above the young man's wrist. "Good boy, Iye." He whispered to the falcon. "Kimama tries to stir up trouble between us."

For her part, Kimama made a business of ignoring Akando's flirtations with the bird, choosing instead to shade her eyes and survey the landscape that surrounded them. She stood in her stirrups for a better view.

"It came over that hump so low it must've hit close around here."

"Think it was a meteor?"

"I think so. Let's try down there."

They continued to follow the riverbed along a course that eventually brought them to the top of a small rise from where they could look down into a shallow valley.

Kimama squinted and pointed. "There. Something silvery. Do you see it?"

He sighted along the line of her finger and then let out a whoop. "Let's check it out."

He started off at a gallop.

"Wait, Akando! We don't know what it is!"

As Akando rushed down the slope toward the machine and its possible unknown dangers, Kimama hurried after him, and finally caught up with him near the top of a rock-strewn incline.

She grabbed him by the arm.

"It could be dangerous. Maybe it's some kind of a bomb."

From where they had stopped, they could look down upon a metallic cubical object, standing erect on tripod legs at the center of a burnt circle on the ground.

Their horses took them at a walk down the hillside to within a bit more than fifty yards of the thing, obviously a machine of sorts, blinking all over with colored lights and sweeping dozens of spiky antennae through the air.

Kimama turned her mount sideways and twisted a bit in the saddle.

"What is it, Akando?"

"Maybe one of those space satellite things crashed."

Kimama dismounted. "It doesn't look like it crashed. One way to find out."

Akando hopped down beside her and secured the falcon to his saddle horn. "Stay, Iye."

Then, as the two of them began a cautious approach to the Machine, a ruby light washed over them from head to foot.

Akando took a step backward. "What?"

And then the machine spoke to them. "Warning: To avoid possible harm, remain clear of my proximate location."

Akando caught Kimama's arm. "I don't think it likes us, Kimama."

She smiled. "Didn't you notice?"

"What?"

She pointed to his ears. "It spoke to us in Shoshone."

"Damn. You're right. It seemed so natural, I completely missed it."

"C'mon."

He hung back, perhaps overly cautious. "Huh?"

"It's speaks our language, Akando. It must be friendly."

He shook his head. "I dunno, Kimama."

"There might be a reward," she offered with conspiratorial logic.

"Ah ... yes. There actually could be a reward."

With that, she grabbed his hand and tugged him forward. They had, in fact, taken only two more steps, when a frizzy light stream hissed out from the machine and zapped them both, knocking them off their feet.

The machine completely ignored the horses and the falcon.

Chapter 8
"Something Rotten in Maryland"

From the air, the complex looked much like any other compound of the Eastern-establishment super wealthy.

Three outdoor pools and two tennis courts beckoned invitingly from amongst unfenced and gently-rolling acres full of low hills, all carpeted with emerald green lawns that even embraced a nine-hole golf course, great and sundry copses of trees, a couple of which actually might have qualified, in different surroundings, as being small forests.

The plane that carried Dan, Tiffany and Ricky, expertly piloted by the enigmatic Mister Quigley – no first name as yet proffered by the man, none yet requested by his passengers – came in low and soundlessly over a huge stone house that, except for arrangements of various metal antennae, might well have been lifted straight out of medieval Europe.

There was even a moat and a drawbridge on what Tiffany took to be the southern exposure.

The plane settled smoothly, without any hint of a bounce, onto a narrow, paved airstrip, taxied to a spot on a parallel apron and came to a stop. By that time, an ornate, horse-drawn coach had pulled up alongside and an industrious ground crew had begun unloading the few personal items from a rear compartment.

Tiffany found the choreography most impressive and said so to her father.

He smiled and allowed, "It would greatly disappoint me, Precious, were you not to encounter many such social refinements and other surprises here."

A side door opened, then, and a crewman offered Tiffany his hand. "Welcome to The Maryland Institute For Neurological Dynamics, Human Ethics And Religious Tolerance, Miss Diamond. Please be careful how you step down."

He guided her on her way out of the plane.

"Thank you," she said sweetly. "Uhm … correct me if I'm wrong. But if I kept proper count on the name of this place, I think the initials spell out 'Mind-Heart'."

He grinned and helped her up into the cushy rear sear of the carriage. "You are quite correct, ma'am."

Dan, Ricky and Quigley followed on their own. And as soon as they were all aboard, and without any word or visible signal from the driver, the horses set out at a trot toward the main house.

Tiffany looked around.

"How far from Washington are we?" she wondered.

Quigley answered, "About sixty miles, madam." He pulled the watch again from his vest pocket, and this time, when he opened the case, Tiffany spotted a bas-relief image of a dirigible in flight pressed into the gold.

He studied the instrument's face briefly, then snapped the cover closed again and frowned slightly, apparently not fully satisfied with their time of arrival.

"Nice watch," offered Tiffany.

Quigley absently wound the watch with a small key. "The others will already be waiting."

As the carriage wheeled around a shallow curve in the road, Tiffany chanced to glance back toward the airstrip in time to see a tall, handsome blonde-haired man descend from a second plane that had just then stopped and stilled its propellers in front of the hanger building.

She thought to herself, "He seems so familiar looking; but I just can't quite – . Actually, if I thought it was at all possible, I'd suspect that might be Senator Frank Farrell. Nah ... no way it could be."

So she turned back toward the front of the coach as it continued in the direction of the main building.

Chapter 9
"Hot Spot"

The coach carrying Tiffany, her father, her cameraman, Ricky and Quigley, crossed the moat and made it safely through the main gate, past the imposing parapets on either side, without having boiling oil poured over them.

They rolled to a stop moments later at the front entrance of the impressive mansion house, its façade, except where the windows and doors interceded, completely covered with thickly woven vines of ivy.

And immediately a small contingent of silent and uniformed staff appeared to escort them up to the stone veranda. They had ascended to a point about halfway up the chiseled front steps, when the approaching clatter of hooves in the cobble stone forecourt below turned Tiffany around in time to see the mystery man from the other plane alight and start up behind them.

She touched Quigley's arm and asked, "Who is that man who arrived in the other plane?"

Quigley only pointed toward the main double doors that opened off the top landing. "This way, Madam."

He escorted them through the front doors in something close to a quick-time march step.

Ø

"Everyone inside, quickly," grumped Quigley impatiently, and with great dispatch, he herded Tiffany, Dan and Ricky into the cavernous front hall.

Once they cleared the threshold, the great oak doors banged shut behind them with a curiously unsettling finality.

Nor were they allowed to tarry there and admire the way the sunlight fell through an amazing stained glass dome overhead, or the massive art pieces of oil and marble, even two full suits of armor.

"There will be time for the cultural tour after the work is finished," he told them as he propelled each one in turn -- by means of unsuspected physical strength applied to the arm just above the elbow – toward a broad marble staircase that that filled most of the room's opposite end.

By the time they reached the tightly shuttered mezzanine level, Ricky had shifted the camera bag several times between his two hands and Dan was actually panting.

It was, also, at that point that they encountered their first genuine surprise since arriving. Electric lights shone from antique fixtures and various staff members operated a number of disparate electrical appliances, including at least one vacuum cleaner.

Dan looked at Quigley. "The crisis is over?"

Instead of answering, Quigley pointed to a door that led off to one side. And to Tiffany and Ricky, he said, "Madam, Mister Ricky, if you would please wait in there."

Tiffany planted her feet firmly. "'Bout time, don't you think, that you said what's going on?"

No hint of telltale expression crossed Quigley's face. He simply took the two of them, one firmly caught in each hand, and compelled them quickly into the designated room.

"You will be very comfortable," he promised, as he shut the door behind them.

Ø

After Quigley had locked the door and dropped the key into the side pocket of his three-piece suit, he turned to Dan and said, "If my actions seem heavy-handed, sir, I do apologize.

When Dan looked a bit anxiously at the door, Quigley added, "But we do have an obligation to keep all of this under very strict wraps; and your daughter and the man with the camera are unexpected additions to our guest list."

Dan nodded slightly.

"Tiffany has always been headstrong. It makes her an excellent reporter, and sometimes, a bit of a pain in the neck. I've on occasion wished I could do what you just did; but it just didn't seem right, being her father, you see?"

"Yes sir," Quigley replied. "In any event, they will be quite safe until we return." He pointed toward the other side of the upper hallway. "Now, if you'll just come this way The others will be waiting.."

"Are you permitted to tell me who these others are?" Dan wondered. He quickly decided the answer must have been a negative, as with considerable dispatch, Quigley guided him to the extreme opposite side of the landing. Once there he hurried Dan into a vintage elevator cage, pressed a button and watched as an electric winch drew the car and its passenger upward.

Only then, with apparent satisfaction, did Quigley turn and retrace his steps back down to the entry hall, arriving at the base of the staircase at precisely the same instant the front doors opened again and Frank Farrell entered.

"Congressman Farrell. You made very good time."

"It's a pleasure to see you again, Mister Quigley. I'm sure your employer told you how important it is that I remain out of sight."

Quigley nodded. "There is a place of adequate concealment from where you can watch and hear everything."

He turned to face an antique settle, which folded away at his touch to reveal an unexpected doorway.

Quigley led Frank inside.

The portal vanished at once behind them.

Chapter 10
"Hospitality Sweet"

The elevator carrying Dan stopped; and Neil E Sepaca, tall, ageless, dashing, retracted the gate to let him out.

"Mister Diamond. Welcome. Would you please come this way?"

As they walk, Dan made no attempt to hide his interest in the trappings along the way.

"Nice place you've got here, Mister Sepaca."

"We do manage to eke out a tolerable existence," Sepaca replied in a well-modulated baritone that carried no hint of any discernable accent. He pointed. "Through that doorway, if you please."

They crossed into an elegant room mainly defined by mirrored walls and a long, polished table.

Plenty of company waited for them there. Small groupings of at least three dozen men and women watched from small, scattered groupings as Dan and Sepaca made their entry.

Immediately the ambient chatter ceased and all but twelve of the room's occupants hastily, noiselessly departed and sealed the doors behind them.

Chapter II
"Tunnel Visions"

Tiffany tried the door in the room where Quigley had exiled them. "Locked. From the outside."

Ricky had been snooping about the various nooks and crannies, opening drawers, examining the contents of several floor to ceiling bookcases. "Whoever owns this place sure reads a lot."

From one shelf he took up a photograph, which obviously had some meaning for him.

"Tiffany?"

"Did you hear me? We're locked inside here, with no way out."

He held up the photo. "Do you know who this man in the picture is?"

She made herself look and answered in an irritable voice. "Uhm ... I guess he does look a little bit familiar."

"He should be more than a <u>little</u> familiar."

She looked again, with gathering interest.

Ricky groaned.

"It's Neil Sepaca."

She moved to his side, lifted the photo from his hand.

"The ...?"

Ricky nodded. "<u>The</u>.

"What the hell's going on here?!" She charged for the door. "It's time we got some answers!"

37

She pounded hard on the molded panels. "Hey. Somebody. Unlock this damned door!"

Ø

Following a flashlight beam through a mostly-dark and narrow passageway, Quigley guided Frank around a gentle curve between the rough-stone walls. He seemed to know when he had reached exactly the right spot. He stopped abruptly and signaled for silence. Then he uncovered a small opening and indicated that Frank should look through it.

In the ceiling of the conference room below, Frank's eye replaced a single star in a mural painted with suns and galaxies, beneath which Dan, Sepaca and the other occupants gathered at one end of a long table.

Neil Sepaca was making introductions.

"Dan, I think you already know Mister Fishbourne."

Even through the peephole high overhead, it was easy to read the hostile body language between the Dan and the dark and skinny young man Sepaca had just identified as Philo "Fish" Fishbourn.

Dan's angry voice drifted up. "Yeah ... he's the sorry son-of-a-bitch that helped ACRONYM steal MindMeld from me."

Fish seemed to make a point of turning his back on Dan. He replied over his shoulder. "Still looking for little green men, Dan?"

His point might have been stronger, had he not been brushed off balance by the passing of an imposing woman wearing an Air Force officer's uniform, complete with bird colonel brasses, as she approached the two men.

"Watch it!" snarled Fish.

Colonel Alison Strong ignored him. "Don't let the little weasel mess with you, Dan'l," came her raspy alto voice, in a level that matched her no-nonsense face.

"Alison!" Dan piped back with genuine delight. He turned to Sepaca. "Alison here actually saw a formation of UFOs."

She growled a slight menace.

"Cost me my star, too."

Sepaca slapped her lightly on one shoulder. "Might be some who already regret that decision, Colonel." He caught another of the attendees by the elbow and drew him into the forming circle. "This is Doctor Alvin Farrell."

Farrell, tall and thin, shook Dan's hand. His voice came out reedy when he said, "I read 'Angels From The Stars'."

Dan's pleasure shown through quite obviously, even from where Frank watched overhead. His voice came across strongly as well and full of humor, "You and about five other people."

After that, Sepaca went around the table.

"That's Natalie Misaka from M.I.T.; Ursula Fontaine, Oxford; Paul Grigsby, J.P.L.; Louise Padget, White Sands; Joel Shank, Sony; Hans Odenwelder, DeuchRadio; Hollis Cryer, Earthstar; and Zipper."

Dan took a tentative step toward the youthful figure with spiked hair. The boy also had numerous piercings and a veritable comic strip of tattoos running up and down his forearms.

"Your name is Zipper?"

The kid waved shyly from low along his body. "I write video games for BLAST-COM."

"Nice to meet you, Zipper."

With that, Sepaca motioned toward the table. "Right. Let's get to work."

Chapter 12
"Tempers, Tempers"

Tiffany kicked the door and winced. Then with a slight limp, she stepped back from the threshold and scanned the room, her eyes stopping on the light fixture suspended from the ceiling. She pursed her lips thoughtfully, and looked across their place of confinement to where Ricky continued to search the bookcases and sundry drawers.

"Ricky?"

He responded without looking at her. "Uh-huh?"

"The lights work, and that vacuum cleaner out in the hallway worked."

This time he turned in her direction.

"Yep."

"Did you ever think to wonder if your camera might work, too?"

He made a small surprised face, scooped up the camera and flipped a switch.

"You're right ... it's back."

She fairly bounded across the room. "All right!" She grabbed a microphone from Ricky's camera bag. "If we can't bust out, we can do what we do best. How do I look?"

"Awful."

"Good. Anytime."

He brought the viewfinder up to his right eye and triggered the record button. "Rolling."

She looked into the camera lens.

"I'm Tiffany Diamond. And along with my cameraman, Ricky Escobar, I'm being held prisoner at Neil Sepaca's country estate outside Washington, a site that houses his famous Mind-Heart Institute."

Ø

Upstairs, in the conference room beneath the celestial ceiling mural with Frank's eye glued to the opposing side of the peephole, the dozen invited guests sat around the table, eyes on Sepaca, who stood before a huge painting of what had to be an imaginary, decidedly alien landscape.

"As agreed," Sepaca reminded them, "there can be no hard copies and no notes. Graphics are available on the REX frames in front of each of you."

Frank watched and listened as Sepaca began to tell his tale.

"In 1953, my father was a technician at White Sands."

The dozen folk around the table shuffled uneasily.

Alice Strong leaned forward. "Are you trying to tell us your father was at Roswell?"

Sepaca visibly squared his shoulders. "I'm saying he actually went inside the ship."

A buzz of excited voices drifted up through the peephole to Frank's ears.

Sepaca swung the painting out from the wall and fiddled with an I.D. pad on a recessed safe.

Dan looked across at Alison Strong. "Guess we're not all that nuts after all, huh?"

As Sepaca opened the safe door, he looked at Dan. "Your bosses at Project Blue Book lied to you, Dan, just like they lied to the rest of us ... to the whole world."

Fish snorted. "Next you'll say pigs can sing opera."

Alison Strong offered, "I once knew a porker named 'Carmen'."

A few sniggers ruffled the air.

Fish glared.

But by then all eyes had moved back to Sepaca, as he reached into the safe a took out a metal box measuring, perhaps a foot long, four inches around.

With a purposeful, dramatic flair, he set the box on the table.

"We have invited Mister Fishbourn to join our select group in order that we might enjoy the benefit of a resident skeptic. But I ask you, for the next few minutes, please believe everything I tell you is the truth."

He lifted the box lid and extracted an object wrapped in some species of ephemeral blue film.

"You've all seen the lights in the sky. They are a type of field generator, designed by our alien visitors to rob us of the things most important to our modern civilization."

He unsealed the blue wrap and slowly peeled it away to reveal a strip of something dull and black.

"Look familiar?"

Thin golden lines traced the object's smooth surface and connected larger patches of the same gold stuff. Sepaca handed the piece to Hans Odenwelder, an intense Black man, whose German accent trembled as he held the item and identified it. "It ... it is clearly ... an ... an integrated circuit."

He passed it to Hollis Cryer.

"Not like any I've ever seen."

Sepaca walked behind their chairs, following the piece as it progressed around the table.

"My father slipped it up his pant leg, carried it out in his sock."

Cryer handed the strip to Paul Grigsby, who whistled between his front teeth. "It's alien? You're sure?"

"I am quite certain."

As Sepaca took a seat at the head of the table, Fish frowned at the strip and gave it to Joel Shank, who cupped it in his palms and asked Sepaca, "You back engineered it?"

"Easily."

Dan scooted back his chair, stood and leaned over the table, resting on one hand, staring hard into Sepaca's eyes. "And, were any of the aliens alive?"

Silence hung heavily in the room for ten seconds or more. No one moved. No one spoke. It seemed, in their being so still, that they did not even breathe.

Finally, in a very soft voice, all the more powerful for its lack of drama, Sepaca said, "Oh ... they were very much alive."

A chair squeaked.

Shank cleared his throat.

Dan sank back into his seat and vigorously rubbed the bridge of his nose.

"My god ... they were alive."

Sepaca seemed to see dust spots on the table. He brushed at them with his left hand. "In fact," he said, "they are all still alive; though one is very sick."

Someone sobbed, perhaps for joy, perhaps in fear.

It was, in fact, Zipper, holding the strip, turning it around in his fingers, smiling at it, who finally broke the spell.

"Cool."

Chapter 13
"Inside Story"

Ricky kept the camera on Tiffany as she picked up the photo of Sepaca and held it in front of her.

"While it would seem that the rest of the world continues to stumble about in paralyzing darkness, this man's home is filled with light and comfort."

Ricky leaned away from the viewfinder, waved her off and lowered the camera.

"Hang on. Batteries're getting low."

He fished a power cord from his bag. "You see an outlet anyplace?"

"Over there."

As Ricky plugged in the cord, he apparently set off something that opened another of the portals, similar to the one in the front entryway.

"What'd I do?"

Tiffany looked through the opening. "You just got us out of here." As she stepped through to the other side, he heard her say, "Bring the camera!"

Ricky followed her with his video and sound equipment.

Ø

Hollis Cryer still held the amazing chip, more to the point, he gripped it tightly with both of his hands, like a selfish child, unwilling to share it with the others there in the conference room.

Neil Sepaca had already circled the table to Cryer's chair, where he tapped the man gently on the shoulder and held out his upturned palm. "Doctor Cryer."

Reluctantly, Cryer surrendered the chip; and as Sepaca rewrapped it and placed it back inside the metal box, he said, "The crash and this strip of alien technology, are but two small parts of an elegant trap."

"But –" sputtered Fontaine "– you said the aliens were real."

Padget nodded vigorously. "Yes, now you've got me confused, too."

Above them, inside the secret hiding space, Frank watched through the view hole and nodded. "Join the club."

Sepaca's voice came up clearly from the room below. "They think we're dangerous."

All eyes, including Frank's, were glued on Sepaca, as he said two words, "Nuclear weapons."

Colonel Strong nodded, "And space travel."

"Exactly," said Sepaca, "coupled with a retrograde spirituality."

And for the first time, Zipper piped up a bit softly at first, quickly gaining enthusiasm as he went on. "Jeez. They hacked into us, dude, and then dumped us back into a techno ice age. Beautiful irony."

Fish pulled a face that suggested a foul odor in the room. He sneered at Zipper. "Are you stoned?"

Zipper shook his head and smiled agreeably. "You bring something?" Then he looked back to Sepaca who had just then finished re-depositing the chip in the safe. "Bet if we could worm a hole in one of those generator thingys, we could ride the link back to mission control and make those guys squeal like a bunch of sick kitties."

Fish actually flinched, visibly. "I'm pretty sure that's not English."

As Sepaca turned the landscape picture so that it lay flat against the wall once more, he looked coolly at Zipper and said, "You'd better hope it works that way."

Ø

Surprisingly nearby, high up inside the dimly-lit tunnel that led from the room where Tiffany and Ricky had, until just recently been held prisoners, the two of them heard a strangely familiar voice say, "Because failing that optimistic scenario, Mister Zipper, your generation will spend from now on just reinventing the wheel."

"Listen, " she whispered.

As Ricky cocked his head, Dan's voice reached them along the passage. "I think Zipper's on the right track."

"There," said Ricky. "I definitely heard somebody talking."

Tiffany picked up the pace. "That was my father's voice."

Ø

As Sepaca resumed his seat at the head of the table, Fish looked straight across at Dan and demanded, "Don't tell me you actually gonna call this bug Zipper."

"Hey, that's my name!" barked the tattooed boy. "And I might've, once in a while, when I wasn't exactly sure what I was doing, eaten a bug or two. But I have never for a fact been one."

Fish measured the young man with undisguised contempt.

"All of which makes me wonder then, what for the love of all that's decent in the universe is that disgusting graffiti you've painted all over your arms?"

Alison Strong raised her hands.

"Gentlemen."

"Aw, he's dissin' my 'tats', lady, uh … I mean Colonel Lady. What I'm saying is these beauties got themselves inked in by some of the greatest skin artists in the world."

"Wonderful," sneered Fish. "So I'm guessing then that your mother must be real proud whenever you show up for a Thanksgiving holiday or whatever."

Zipper wavered and dipped his eyes for the first time.

"Maybe she might be, I guess, except I think she's probably dead, since I'm adopted."

"Aw … " breathed Alison Strong.

But Zipper came back, seized by a sudden inspiration.

"Oh … all right. Here's how it is. From now on, every time you're rude to me, I'm gonna call you, 'Flash'."

"Now you listen --!"

Alison Strong tried again to restore order.

"Hey ... children –"

But by that time, Zipper was too furious with Fish to hold his tongue.

"You won't say my name right."

"On some rare occasions, I allow my friends – of which you definitely are not one – to call me 'Fish'! But for the likes of you, it will forever be 'Mister Fishbourn'!"

"Yeah? That's fine. And you, for being so nasty, can address my tats as 'Mister Doodles'; and then you can kiss both my rear cheeks."

Everybody laughed, obviously in sympathy with Zipper.

Fish was suitably chagrined.

"Not very damned likely."

A near-deafening shriek shuddered the room then. The occupants trembled visibly and covered their ears. Colonel Alison Strong had just whistled through her front teeth.

"All right ... 's gone on long enough boys. Best save the rest of it for the bad guys."

And at that same time, almost directly overhead, Tiffany and Ricky approached a sharp curve in the passageway. And once again, her father's voice floated up to them, clearer this time.

"As I was saying, those generators really could be a way to take the battle right back to the aliens."

Around the conference table, Fish leaned forward and set his eyes accusingly on Sepaca.

"Or maybe we should just work out a deal with the aliens, like our host apparently has."

Sepaca opened his mouth to reply; but again, Dan stepped in. "Why not just say it plain, Fish."

Fish seemed on the verge of answering back. But before the words could form in his mouth, Sepaca said, "Mister Fish is wondering why I, alone, have power for my home."

"Lots of exceptions," volunteered Dan Farrell. My pacemaker's working; and so is the critical equipment at my local hospital."

"It does all seem pretty damn selective," agreed Alison Strong. "The best we know is that all in-flight aircraft made it down okay before losing power."

Chapter 14
"Primordial Poop"

As Tiffany and Ricky approached yet another turn in the maze-like passage walls, the voices that drew them on, especially the ones raised in anger or heated defense, came with ever greater clarity up from the conference room that by that time lay directly below the passageway.

Tiffany brought a finger to her lips and the two of them tiptoed forward. They would not have known it was Sepaca's words they heard.

"Six months ago, we pick up the first alien warnings. At that point there would have been plenty of time to shield our cities. But the stubborn politicians would not believe that the threat was real."

The voice still echoed as Tiffany finished the turn just ahead of Ricky and spotted Dan bent over the spy hole.

"Congressman Farrell!"

Twelve pair of eyes in the room right beneath her jumped from Sepaca's face to the mural in the ceiling, from which Tiffany's voice continued to resonate.

The alto voice came again from on high. "I thought I recognized that famous profile."

Her father gasped. "Tiffany?"

Fish stood and pointed at Sepaca. "You promised us security, damn it!"

Padget pointed at the mural. "Something just moved up there. I'm sure I saw it."

The movement Padget saw had resulted when Frank Farrell withdrew his eye from the peephole and replaced the glass plug.

Frank and Quigley turned to face Tiffany and Ricky.

"How did you get here?" demanded Quigley in a hoarse whisper, a level of forced restraint that had quickly turned his face beet red.

Frank smiled at Tiffany and, after signaling her to an impatient silence, whispered to Quigley, "I've seen enough."

Quigley glared at Tiffany and led the way toward the mouth of a different passage. The others fell in at once behind him.

Chapter 15
"New Contracts"

With the exception of Zipper, the desturbance from right over their heads had brought everyone in the conference room to their feet.

Almost everyone.

Zipper alone remained seated, leaned back in his chair, legs outstretched, fingers laced casually behind his head, staring upward at the ceiling.

Standing next to him, Sepaca had launched into an unenviable attempt at trying to restore some useful measure of calm to the assembly.

"Please, I assure you, you are in absolutely no danger."

Zipper pointed straight up. "I think the hole was right up there in the Phoenix Constellation."

Louise Padget agreed. "Yes, it's gone now; but the hole definitely was in that star system right there!"

Fish went so far as to leave his chair and start toward the door. "If Dan's snoopy TV daughter is here, we are absolutely in the greatest of all possible peril."

"Hey!" yelled Dan, as he started after Fish. "I've put up with a lot from you, but I will not for even an instant tolerate your insulting my daughter's good name and professionalism!"

"Gentlemen ... gentlemen ... please, ladies, everyone," entreated Sepaca. "In fact Miss Diamond is a guest on the estate. But she is confined to another wing of the house."

Fish charged back toward the table. "We heard her voice, Sepaca!"

"It's a very old house, Mister Fishbourn. "Strange acoustics. We must adopt a course of action. Ladies, gentlemen, retake your seats, please."

In the strained silence that followed, they all seemed to be taking stock, surveying the room, with special attention directed toward the ornate ceiling. Nothing moved. There came not the slightest bump or scrape. The only sound was their quiet breathing. And as several more uneventful seconds passed, the overall panic slowly subsided.

"Please," coaxed Sepaca in the calmest possible tones. "At all cost, we must prevail in our mission."

And after just a bit of further hesitation, and in the absence of any fresh distractions from outside the room, Padget and Odenwelder slowly returned to their chairs, and one by one, the others grudgingly did the same.

Fish was the last among them to take his place; and he took his time doing it.

Sepaca exhaled hard. "Good. My deepest thanks."

Ø

Quigley opened a door in the passageway and Frank, Tiffany and Ricky stepped out into the main entry hall.

Tiffany waited patiently until the opening behind the settle had reclosed itself; then she said to Frank, "You don't really seem to be playing with the other little boys and girls."

He smiled, genuinely amused. "I find that sometimes I work more effectively on my own. I don't suppose I could persuade you to join our little group."

Quigley looked genuinely horrified at the prospect. "Sir."

Tiffany laughed softly. "Don't concern yourself unnecessarily, Mister Quigley." And to Frank she said, "The offer, though vague, intrigues me. But like you, Congressman, I work most effectively on my own."

Frank gave her a brief, mock pout. "I need someone I can trust to chronicle these events for later generations."

"Sir!" sputtered Quigley.

"Yes Quigley, I know," Frank said with a half a chuckle. And to Tiffany he added, "Your country needs you. The world needs you." He paused and leaned in conspiratorially close to her. "Complete access."

She laughed out loud. "I'm not sure I like being thought of as trustworthy."

"Too late. Your reputation precedes you."

Chapter 16
"Thieves In The Night"

Sepaca picked up a pair of the REX frames from off the conference and adjusted them to fit his face.

"The alien base for this intervention is being directed from an artificial planetoid first sighted between the orbits of Neptune and Pluto a little more than eighteen months ago."

The others all donned the lens-less frames, which began at once to project laser images directly onto their retinae.

Dan was the last to slip his on. What he, and presumably the others, saw was a small, glistening metal ball rotating slowly and drawing nearer.

As they watched, Sepaca continued to narrate the visuals. "Earth scientists named it 2000 EB173. It is now orbiting a bit more than three hundred miles above the earth, with the most obvious effect being small changes in tidal patterns."

He touched a miniature control unit clipped to his collar.

"Some cultures around the globe, such as Mennonite, Native American, Amish, because they are self-sufficient, have hardly noticed any change at all in the way they live their lives."

Fish looked at Sepaca over the tops of his frames. "Did I fall asleep and miss the part where somebody put you in charge?"

"As you so aptly observed, Mister Fishbourn, I'm the only one who has any power. If you can match that, I'll gladly relinquish the authority. And you would know better than the rest of us if you have fallen asleep."

Every eye watches Fish. He tightened his lips briefly then readjusted his frames.

An animated map inside the REX presentation began to sprout red markers.

"We'll work out of the type of independent sites I've just mentioned," Sepaca told them. "They all lie well away from the urban collapse. The aliens have given us a week – reckoned from Greenwich – to settle our conflicts of interest and solve this puzzle. One day's nearly gone."

Fish lowered his frames again. "Wait. They sent demands? In clear text?"

"Clear as the technology they used to bait the trap in the first place. For security's sake you're each seeing only your personal assignments and base of operation."

The graphics from the REX formed fresh charts inside all their eyes.

"I've teamed you up so your specialties compliment one another. Dan, I've linked you and Alison for space flight and military liaison."

Sepaca touched the lapel control again. "Professor Farrell and Doctor Fontaine, Shank and Odenwelder, Padget-Cryer, Misaka-Grigsby."

"Hold on!" Fish stood up so fast his chair fell over. "That leaves only me and the Zipper, here. You're not teaming me with him!"

Ø

Fish jerked off his REX frames; and in short order, he had made his way around the table to a point where he stood directly behind Natalie Misaka's chair.

More to the point, he was yelling at Sepaca.

"If you intention was to insult me, you have succeeded beyond your wildest dreams!"

"I don't understand," soothed Sepaca. "You're both software experts and, dare I say, voodoo hackers."

"I don't work with freakoids!"

For the second time, Zipper seemed genuinely stung both by Fish's choice of words and general attitude.

"Aw, Dude."

Fish kept his dark eyes fixed on Sepaca, but pointed accusingly at Zipper.

"You hear that? '<u>Dude</u> this, <u>dude</u> that!' Would anybody else in this room be willing to work with the likes of him?"

As if he expected negative responses from the others, Zipper rested his hands on the table in front of him, brought the opposing finger tips together and seemed to study the result in a rather shy manner.

And indeed there did follow a prolonged silence in the room, as everyone present seemed to be thinking about Fish's question

After a moment, Alvin Farrell raised his hand.

"I would, if Mister Sepaca's right about Zipper's abilities."

Zipper looked up with a surprised smile.

"Me, too," said Hollis Cryer.

Ursula Fontaine added her voice, "Same here."

And all the others raised their hands as well.

Zipper whispered a surprised, "Thank you."

Fish stood there, obviously stunned.

And Sepaca's voice, rolling out softly, cooly into the ensuing silence, could not have offered much comfort.

He said, "Fine, Mister Fishbourn. If you really want to watch humankind's greatest adventure from the sidelines, Quigley can fly you home." He glanced at his watch. "You could be airborne within fifteen minutes." He paused and let the words hang. "Or you can stay attached to our group and work with Zipper."

Fish's jaw slackened. "You value him over me?!"

"In fact, Mister Fishbourn, I have selected every one of you with great care, each for a very special reason. So I place exactly the same value on each member of all of the five teams."

Slowly Fish closed his mouth, searched the faces of all those other eyes turned on him. When he found no appearance of support, he slowly righted his chair, set the frames back on his nose and reseated himself in much the same posture as he had been before his outburst.

Sepaca let the silence hang for another moment. Then he picked up the briefing as if nothing at all had happened.

"You will all have laser phones equipped with shielded power cells."

Dan raised his hand like a nervous schoolboy and asked if their signal path would be limited to line-of-sight.

"Yes," Sepaca answered. "I'm afraid it's the best we can do. Depending on the terrain, the signal could carry only a few yards or several miles."

He removed his REX frames then and the others followed suit, their eyes riveted on Sepaca.

"Each team will carry a box containing something uniquely vital to that team's mission," he told them. "Whatever you do, you should not open the box until after you've tried everything else."

"Something different for each team?" asked Misaka.

"One common element in all the boxes is an energy cell the size of a chocolate bar. Don't be fooled by its size. It packs the power of a small hydroelectric dam."

"Little something you whipped up in your flying lab?" asked a contrite Fish in as soft a voice as he could muster.

"Sky Haven," offered Strong to no one in particular. "That's what he calls the 'flying lab'."

"The trade off," continued Sepaca, "is life span. Once you break the seal on your team's box, the alien field generators will go to work on it; and they'll drain it completely dry within twenty-four hours."

He checked his watch. "Departure time, thirty minutes."

Chapter 17
"A Scoop of Vanilla"

Outside, with the verdant Maryland countryside spread out before them, Frank, Tiffany, Ricky and Quigley descended the front steps to where one of the horse-drawn coaches waited to take them back to the landing strip.

Quigley, making no effort to disguise his displeasure, marched along in martial stride beside Frank.

"Mister Sepaca will not be pleased."

"I would imagine not, Quigley," Frank agreed with a forced smile. "You should tell him I said, 'If you can't lick 'em, get them to join you'."

He and Tiffany and Ricky made quick business of boarding the coach, which lurched immediately down the drive in the direction of the airstrip.

Ricky checked out his camera and announced. "It's broke again."

"No sweat," said Frank. "We'll get you one of those shielded power cells from the laser radios."

Tiffany smiled at him coyly. "Don't take too long, Congressman, or I may have to rethink our deal."

He returned her smile; and briefly there existed a definite flash of magic between them. Then he grew very serious again.

"I'll keep my part of the bargain, Tiffany. But never forget, your father's involved here, too."

She scowled.

"I sincerely hope that's not some kind of a threat."

"Not a bit of it. But just so you're aware, people could actually die if any of this leaks out."

Chapter 18
"Judas and the Little Boy's Room"

An eye peeked briefly out through a narrow window cut through stone and located high up on the mansion's outside wall.

Although the slit lay almost invisible from outside, it provided a convenient spy hole out through the southern exposure, which was the same one that faced toward the airstrip.

Its limited functionally let faint light into a tiny bathroom, which was something of a secret misfit in its own right, quite obviously jerry-fitted into a nether corner long after the original construction had been completed, its very existence possibly long since forgotten.

Its space was, however, the perfect seclusion for concealing such a grave series of misdeeds as were about to occur there.

That same eye quivered nervously and blinked, then withdrew from the outside light, as a rubber-gloved finger came up to it and tugged the outside corner of its lid. Immediately a contact lens fell into an upturned palm, also, sheathed in latex. A second lens landed near the first.

Thumb and forefinger retrieved the tiny discs and dropped them into a translucent cube that briefly leaked red light.

As the fingers rotated the cube, a small screen on it brightened, and Sepaca's graphics played with the sound of his captured voice.

"Dan, I've linked you and Alison for space flight and military liaison."

The finger pressed a button on one side and the screen image changed to moving patterns, then flashed "MESSAGE SENT".

The hand pocketed the transmitter box and produced a larger box with a digital timer, which counted down from twenty minutes. Strong magnets on the box stuck it to the wash basin's underside.

Ø

Professor Farrell and Ursula Fontaine carried a red metal box past one of the wind-up planes, where Natalie Misaka and Paul Grigsby loaded another box of identical color and design into the cargo bay.

Dan, Tiffany and Ricky left their carriage and walked to another craft, where a man wearing aviator's goggles, a leather helmet and a long scarf waited beside the door.

"Good afternoon," said the strangely attired fellow. "They call me 'Goggles'."

His three passengers exchanged quizzical looks, then quickly climbed on board.

One of the planes was already launching itself skyward; and two more had lined up on the runway for their turn.

All the activity was clearly visible from a balcony of the Mind-Heart mansion, where Sepaca and Quigley watched one of the planes whistle low over the roof top.

"Was there a transmission?" Sepaca asked Quigley.

Quigley checked his pocket watch. "Eight minutes ago."

"Do we know who sent it?"

"Could have been any one of them."

"And a bomb?"

"Just as you expected."

The shadow of another plane dashed across them.

"That would be the last of the staff, sir."

Sepaca turned from the railing.

"Then it's time we took our leave, too, Quigley."

"A highly commendable idea, sir."

The last remaining plane climbed quickly off the airstrip and banked sharply away from the estate. It had gone only a short distance when an enormous fireball leaped from the mansion's roof and poured out its windows like liquid hell.

Sepaca rode beside Quigley, who manned the controls. The plane shuddered briefly as the explosion's shock wave rolled over it.

"I might not mind so much if we knew who betrayed us," offered Sepaca.

"No, sir."

"Still," Sepaca said with more than a touch of regret in his voice. "There can be no doubt who arranged it."

... part two

"Stretch out thine hand toward heaven,
that there may be darkness over the land of Egypt,
even darkness which may be felt."
Exodus 10:21

Chapter I
"City of Lights"

Under rain-filled skies, a sectioned, ebony snake-like thing raced past ancient picture-postcard villages nestled beside tree-lined river banks. The thing's shock wave whipped tall grass bordering the right of way.

It was, that thing, a machine of some human construct, led along a shallow trench by a needle-shaped engine that bore a logo reading: "ACRONYM".

Within the metallic shell, four grim-faced guards, all heavily armed, bracketed a door of polished wood.

Behind that door. inside a posh carriage, a particular light blinked insistently. A hand touched a button; and a large wall screen lit up to show Neil Sepaca at the head of his conference table.

Sepaca's voice filled the hurtling cocoon. "Obviously we cannot have any hard copies floating around. I've teamed you up so your specialties compliment one another."

On through the slash of storm and lightning went the incredible engine, the special coach and others dragged pell-mell behind it.

Flashing near a squatters' encampment filled with thin and dirty people, the train's passing blew the nearest tent off its supports and scattered its miserable occupants.

Ø

Thunder and fire ruled the skies over the world's most beautiful city.

Toward the east, the Eiffel Tower cut through the lowest echelons of heaven, even as the ACRONYM maglev neared the Seine River, where Notre Dame Cathedral adorned the Ile de la Cite in midstream. At that very point, the right of way deepened and carried man and machine into an intestinally dark tunnel.

The vibrations lessened as the train's velocity slowed to a judicious crawl, made necessary, most likely, by its transit of the tunnel, soon to surface again in the Cathedral's familiar forecourt, where a large sign proclaimed in French, English, German and five other languages: "Through a special condemnation ruling, this building and its environs have been deconsecrated and are now private property. Trespassers will be shot without additional warning."

The train rose from beneath the river and glided to a precision stop before the cathedral's ornate front entrance.

As soon as the magnetic repulsion had dissipated from its underside, the machine settled onto the track bed and an enclosed passageway reached out and quickly attached itself to the special coach's door. Immediately an indistinct figure moved through the rain-streaked tube directly into the cathedral itself, where massive doors banged shut behind a phalanx of guards.

Boot steps echoed through an empty nave watched over by ancient carved demons from high in the great, vaulted ceiling.

A robbed priest rushed to meet one Ator Guinard, little more than an indistinct figure at the party's center. The procession stopped.

"Sepaca's stronghold lies in ruins," the priest panted excitedly.

Guinard remained tantalizingly screened from view in the guards' shadows. Still his voice came forth like the snap of dried bones. "Ruined, yes. But not before he'd scattered his drones over the entire globe and made quite good his own escape."

As if obeying an unspoken command, the party resumed walking, their whispered stride subdued so as not to compete with Guinard's words. "Find my Chosen One."

The Priest hurried to catch up. "But mightn't that arouse suspicion?"

The guards stopped outside a foreboding portal beneath the altar. Guinard turned slightly, the sharpness of his features catching just a hint of the dim lights. "Do as I tell you."

Then his shadow slid over the ancient threshold and descended stone steps smoothed by centuries of processional footfalls. Downward clicked the hard soles of his shoes, down toward water dripping somewhere in the shadows, on down to the crypt floor and on still through dim patches of light thrown by strings of glowing sconces.

And he stopped finally, alone, surrounded by ancient stone, and throwing back his head, he bellowed to no one in sight, "And yet, Sky Haven still survives!"

Chapter 2
"Gas Bag"

On that particular morning, in the sky above coordinates centered in the Atlantic Ocean about midway between Newfoundland and Ireland, the sky spread flawlessly blue, boringly featureless to the limits of unaided human vision in all directions.

That perfection, certainly the illusion of it, fleeted away quite soon, as a tiny, sometimes-shiny flyspeck cruised into view. Approaching from roughly the west-south-west, the anomaly seemed to follow an intentional heading that might eventually result in its meeting up with a small cloud that had lain too close atop the waves to draw much notice up till that point.

Soon that cloud revealed itself as something more than a mere curiosity.

It rose slowly from its skim on the water and drifted a bit back off its previous northeasterly course in such a fashion as to suggest that it might possibly, within the next ten to twelve minutes, arrive at a point of rendezvous with the airborne speck.

In fact, as the tiny mote grew nearer to the specified spot above the Atlantic, it proved to be one of Sepaca's planes.

It was, by no coincidence, the very same one Quigley had piloted out of the airfield in Maryland only hours earlier.

Quigley remained at its controls, with Sepaca at his side in the front passenger seat.

"You are a remarkable navigator, Quigley."

"Thank you, sir."

"It still amazes me more than a little how you need no compass or satellite-linked instrumentation to find your way about."

"Tis just my nature, sir."

"Of course."

Quigley banked the plane straight toward the cloud. And soon fluffy white replaced blue sky outside the cockpit.

The plane bored deeper into the anomalous white puff and emerged into a clear space surrounding an enormous dirigible, which emitted, from several ports, a white vapor that added to the camouflage. Letters boldly emblazoned on the craft's side spelled out the name SKY HAVEN.

As Sepaca's plane made its approach. the dirigible grew ever larger through the windscreen. Soon a door widened on the gondola beneath the larger craft and the plane slipped deftly inside.

Ø

Filtered sunlight poured in through the mostly-clear upper portions of the dirigible's skin, and fell on Sepaca and Quigley as they exited a futuristic lift and walked along one of several intersecting bridges eight stories up. Laboratories and test chambers offered themselves on every side.

Under his breath, Sepaca said to Quigley, "Have Captain Stackhouse find us some clouds so that we're less conspicuous. And tell him to move us into the trade winds."

From the corners of his eyes, Quigley glanced over at his master.

"Guinard's coming?"

Sepaca nodded. "Very soon now."

Then as Sepaca continued on his way, Quigley veered onto another catwalk that took him by a lush greenhouse. He seemed at first to ignore the flowers inside. But as he passed, his hand snapped out, performed some arcane act of legerdemain, and brought back a snared white carnation for his lapel.

Chapter 3
"How You Gonna Keep 'em?"

Shadowy stands of trees several rows deep lined the right of way along the interstate where it paralleled the western boundary of Seth Burwell's farm.

Mainly the narrow strip of forestry consisted of oaks, all of which carried crowns of rainbow leaves still clinging to their upper branches.

The opening through copses marked the entry to the farm. The trees themselves, as with the customs of its residents, helped shield both farm and family from curious intrusions from the outside world.

The road that lead up from the interstate to the front gate of the Burwell farm was all dirt and gravel. It was, on the other hand, well maintained to the point of showing almost no wear at all. And at the moment, it was probably busier than it ever had been in all its prior existence.

By contrast, the interstate, though it had many cars and trucks on it, sat motionless, as if the motorized monsters, in the process of fleeing some terrible fate had fallen and died while in full flight.

On the Burwell's private road, there was plenty of activity, no fewer than fifty hand and bicycle-drawn carts lined up, with more arriving with every passing minute.

At the very head of the queue there sat a horse-drawn wagon. And nearby, Fish, Seth and Caleb faced one another over a whitewashed gate.

Fish was pulling a folded paper from his shirt pocket. He said to Seth, "I believe you reported to the Sheriff's Department this morning that during the night, some sort of a machine had crashed on your property. Is that right, Mister Burwell?"

Seth nodded cautiously.

"That's about the size of it."

Fish opened the paper and passed it to Seth.

"As you can see, that's an introductory letter from Sheriff Wiley requesting that you let us come onto your land to conduct a proper investigation of the machine and the circumstances of its arrival."

Seth quickly finished reading the letter and brought his eyes back up even with Fish's.

"When you say us, who would that be, in addition to yourself?"

A chirpy voice from behind Fish replied, "That would be me, sir."

Seth did a surprised take.

"What in the world?"

Fish glanced back over his shoulder to find Zipper ambling casually in their direction.

"Could you please tell me, Mister fish, what is that supposed to be?" demanded Seth in a low voice.

Fish shook his head. "That would be Zipper, Mister Burwell. You might want to think of him as my evil twin."

Seth scrunched his face a bit, "And if I let you in, do I have to let this Zipper guy in, too?"

"Yes sir ... it pains me to tell you that for the duration, the two of us are more or less joined at the hip."

Seth visibly thought through all his options, then he opened the gate.

He pointed.

"Contraption's just over that rise."

Zipper led the wagon through. "Nice morning, isn't it, sir?"

Seth looked sidelong at Caleb, who grinned back at him mischievously.

"Thank you, Mister Burwell," said Fish.

"Oh I'm gonna have to let the rest of 'em in anyhow," Seth told him. "Couldn't hardly let 'em sit out here and starve."

Ø

As Seth began supervising the camping arrangements for the new squatters, Caleb lead Fish and Zipper over a hillock to where the machine sat defiantly at the edge of a tree-ringed hollow.

"Whoa!" breathed Zipper. "Way, way cool."

"Be careful," Caleb warned them. "It stings something awful."

Fish nodded. "Not surprised."

"Pa calls it 'Satan's minion'."

"Given what little I know of its function, that would not be a completely unreasonable point of view."

Caleb held back as Fish and Zipper descended the hill to within about two feet inside the burn area, at which point the machine scanned them.

The scan seemed as much a warning as the voice that came with it.

"Warning: to avoid possible harm, remain well clear of my proximate location."

Zipper sniggered. "I like that machine. It's got some real attitude, man."

Caleb yelled down, "It means business, guys!"

"It would help," offered Fish, "if we knew how close it'd let us get."

Zipper nodded. "Okay."

He stepped off blithely toward the machine, managing only a dozen steps before a white beam darted out and laid him flat.

Fish is aghast. "Jeez." He cautiously grabbed one of Zipper's out-flung arms and dragged him back outside the apparent danger zone. "Are you nuts?"

He helped Zipper sit up.

"Are you all right?"

"How close did I get, Dude?"

"Uh ... maybe ten feet."

Zipper grinned and winked at Fish. "Think I've got an idea."

Chapter 4
"Dirty Work"

Twin sprays of dirt seemed to leap up on their own up out of a hole dug about fifteen feet out from where the machine had planted itself. One load landed on Fish's shoes.

Seth glanced back toward the house and spotted Sara coming with a bucket. "Water's on the way."

Fish wiped his mouth in anticipation. "You say she and the boy are twins?"

Seth nodded and, in what was obviously a conspiratorial tone, added, "Different as rain and shine."

Zipper popped his head up out of the hole and saw Sara and the water bucket. He grinned with delight.

"Just in time."

He climbed out of the hole dragging a shovel behind him; Caleb followed, lugging a pickaxe.

Then, as Sara handed Zipper a dripping ladle, their hands touched briefly, and he gave her an interested smile.

"Hi."

She offered him a small nod. "Hello."

Seth stepped quickly between them and said to Zipper, "Tell me again how it's gonna help to dig this hole."

Zipper seemed a bit startled by the man's sudden nearness. "Uhm, well, I'm hoping that protective field may not see us if we come at it from underneath." He handed the ladle back to Sara. "Thanks. Good water."

"You're quite welcome."

"Hmm ... " went Caleb. "But what if the machine does see us?"

"Well then, bro," began Zipper as and jumped back into the pit, "you and me get zapped again."

"Oh great!"

He followed Zipper into the hole and more dirt began coming out.

Chapter 5
"A Dry Heat"

One of Sepaca's wind-up planes, its propeller stuck motionless at twenty minutes past ten o'clock, skimmed a jagged ridge and touched down on the sandy earth.

The craft rolled a bit, then bumped to a stop. And within seconds, Dan Diamond and Alison Strong were climbing out.

Strong pushed the perspiration up away from her eyes. "This's like being one of those early mail pilots, following the telegraph wires."

While she sighted the sun through a sextant-like instrument, Dan pulled the cranks from the plane's storage space.

"I'd be glad if we could go more than a couple hundred miles without a windup."

By that time she had produced a map and was studying the topography.

"Ever hanker to visit Death Valley, Dan'l?"

"That where we are?"

She nodded. "Smack dab." Then she glanced up and turned a full circle, as she surveyed the horizon. And as she came almost completely around, her expression suddenly grew very serious. "And don't look now, but there's Indians behind you."

"Very funny."

"Not if you're on Indian land," said an unexpected third voice.

"Damn!" Dan whirled around and found himself eye-to-eye with Akando, who carried Iye on his shoulder. Kimama had a rifle.

"How much reward for the satellite?" demanded Akando.

Kimama frowned at him and noticed Dan and Strong exchanging surprised glances.

"It's possible, maybe, that the space thing doesn't belong to you," she ventured.

Dan shrugged. "We won't know till we see it."

"How much?" Akando demanded again.

Dan pulled out his wallet. "A hundred dollars?"

Akando pointed to himself and Kimama. "One hundred each."

Dan withdrew two bills and held them out.

Akando said one short word, "Iye"; and the falcon leaped from his shoulder, snatched the money on the fly and carried it back to Akando.

Alison Strong grinned with delight. "Well I'll be blazed."

Kimama and Akando pocketed the money, then turned; and as the two of them walked toward the mouth of a small arroyo, Dan yelled after them, "Hey!"

"Let's go, Dan'l. I get the feeling those two young people want us to follow them."

She and Dan headed out at a fast walk, matching the footprints left in the sand by Kimama and Akando.

Chapter 6
"Who Goes There?"

Hans Odenwelder lay prone and partly tangled up in a stand of scrub brush. All around there were thick formations of pine trees that seemed to go on forever.

And there was, it seemed most definitely, a deadly, mocking chatter afloat in the air. It mixed with a white acrid smoke and hung in thin drifts maybe ten feet off the ground.

Odenwelder was not alone. Not far from him, behind one of the fat tree trunks, Joel Shank cowered in abject terror.

They both had good reason to be afraid.

Heavy automatic weapons fire rattled steadily from a knot of weathered cabins and bunkers set in a clearing, which was surrounded by ten-foot barbed wire fences and guard towers with vintage carbon arc lamps.

Bark splintered and ripped away from the exposed side of trees only inches away from where the two men lay trembling.

Odenwelder spit out a mouthful of ripe forest soil.

"You said this was an old hippie commune."

Shank seemed to be crying. "That's what the damned map says."

"Are you crying?"

"I'm allergic to pine trees."

"Yeah ... okay."

Odenwelder finally freed his coat from a thorny shrub limb, which somehow had traveled most of the way up his right sleeve. He began to crawl off through the underbrush on his belly.

"Where are you going?" demanded Shank.

"Back to the freakin' road."

Shank seemed to decide Odenwelder's plan was a wise one; and he began squirming on his ample stomach, too. But they had covered only a few yards before encountering a formation of camouflaged pant legs neatly tucked into the tops of combat boots.

In near perfect synchronization, Shank and Odenwelder looked up past a dozen rifle muzzles at Commander Jeremiah Magwood, stocky, crew cut, grim-faced. The man's voice carried to the two men's ears a certain ursine snarl.

He said, "Blink, and you're Swiss cheese."

Chapter 7
"Old Salt"

Within the range of normal human vision, blue skies rode endlessly high over equally blue water. Nothing so mundane as dry land of any perceptible size appeared to spoil the view below.

There was but one small disturbance of any sort, a narrow streak of white on the water, a wake plowed by the bow of a beautifully long clipper ship, a modern improvisation of the Cutty Sark.

The vessel, matte black with high-tech metal sails, rode effortlessly fast and majestically high through the wind-tossed foam and spray.

A closer look revealed at mid-ship, between the masts, an elevated pad that held four inky ACRONYM helicopters.

A cart labeled H2N-HN2 rolled away after fueling up one of the choppers. Drops from the fueling hoses splattered drippings from a second cart tagged O2N-NO2, and a brief, hissing flash lit the deck.

The crewmen scattered.

One, slightly burned, yelled a rage at the errant drivers, "Damn it all. How many times I got to say keep them carts at opposite ends of the ship?"

A second crewman checked out the first man.

"Nasty stuff."

"Jeez. That's the beauty of it, how it don't need no spark to burn."

By that time, the carts had left the deck for some nether safety zone. And one by one, the helicopters got the okay to lift off the pad and head away in tight formation.

From the pilot's seat in the cockpit of the lead craft, a trim and youthful Captain Jolly, looked back briefly at the flight deck, then checked the other three choppers in the formation.

To his copilot he said, "Hook us up."

The copilot pulled a short lever on the control panel; and on the outside of the craft, a door popped open and telescoped an arm holding a complex array, one part flat vial filled with green gel, the other a sort of flexible prism.

Immediately upon hitting the air, the vial swiveled to face the sun, positioning the prism to catch the light and direct it at the other choppers.

Jolly brought a microphone to his mouth. "Stalker Commander to Blue, Yellow, Red."

Outside, Jolly's words vibrated the prism which scrambled the sunlight spectrum, then reflected the patterns to the other helicopters, where they crews heard Jolly say, "Lock and load munitions and test fire for accuracy."

Briefly the choppers burp gunfire.

Jolly's voice said, "Okay. Let's go find Sky Haven."

Chapter 8
"In Seine"

If one listened closely, there was, quite audible, the gurgle and splash of the Seine relayed through the ancient stone embankment.

Perhaps from the river, perhaps from the undisturbed age of the place, there hung a dank odor, a sensual patina so strong it seemed almost visible to the unaided eye.

Centuries before its current occupants arrived to build the cathedral, that same stench had clung close to the roughly hewn walls in the structure's rotting bowels, wherein, at that moment, lay Guinard's crypt.

Yet, it seemed the very essence of the lone figure standing trance-still in the dusky green light, dark eyes turned toward a cold shimmer that rose off the dozen computer readouts arrayed beneath his quickly moving hands.

Liquid light ripped, too, off some nearby agitated pool in some unimportant niche that might have served some long-forgotten purpose.

The figure raised his uncommon head the smallest degree in certain response to the approach of tentative footfalls down the hard steps.

Those reluctant slaps, hollow, on the edge of retreat, carried with them the echo of certain failure.

Guinard did not actually turn around as the Priest came slowly nearer and hovered just beyond harm's reach. Wisely, the frightened cleric said nothing.

He waited uncertainly until Guinard's voice rasped at him like thin metal.

"Is the strike force away?"

The Priest shivered.

"Just now, sir."

"And have you located my Chosen One?"

The Priest wheezed in the brief silence, as if he were trying to force himself to say something he already regretted.

Still Guinard did not turn.

"I hope your silence does not tell me you have failed."

"Oh ... Sir. Discretion, security, it is most difficult."

Guinard whirled suddenly, his raised right arm ending in a glowing spine, which he brought down hard across the Priest's unfortunate face. The man screamed and fell to the floor sobbing.

"By now," rasped Guinard, "you must surely know that I never indulge myself in the difficulties an underling might encounter in the execution of my instructions."

The head did finally turn then so that a stray path of the dimmest light made slashes over a deviant protrusion on Guinard's forehead. The spine, which had seemed a permanent fixture of the hand itself, fell yet again.

"Please, sir, please!" cried the poor fellow all twisted and twitching there on the floor. He looked up at his master through fingers that dripped fresh blood.

"Leave my presence, you thing of worthless pity! Go!"

The Priest, only too happy to have gained his leave, scrambled to his feet and ran for the stairs. As his footfalls faded, Guinard turned back to the console.

And in an apparent oral note to himself, he said, "We should long ago have left them in the trees."

Chapter 9
"Machine Politics"

Sand and loose bits of ephemeral matter blew in small, tight circles, braded by devious currents that skated, mostly unhindered, down the wasted plain.

Directly Kimama and Akando came into view around a rock formation with Dan and Strong puffing along behind.

In a hoarse whisper, Dan told Strong, "They're trying to give us heart attacks."

"They're half our age, Dan'l."

"Which would make us each a quarter of your combined age," offered Kimama over her shoulder.

She and Akando stopped abruptly; and she pointed.

"There."

The machine waited no more than forty feet away.

"Good lord," whispered Dan.

Then, as he and Strong advanced slowly on the machine, Akando looked at Kimama and grinned mischievously. She shook her head at him and called after Dan and Strong, "Stop."

Akando breathed out, "Shit!"

"What is it?" asked Strong.

Kimama sighed. "If you get too close, it hurls lightning at you."

Strong nodded at Kimama. "Thank you for the warning."

Then, as Kimama and Akando looked on, Strong and Dan walked a series of orbits around the machine. The third time, the two Indians joined them.

Kimama wondered, "Will you take it away?"

Strong replied that such an endeavor might be impossible, if they could not even touch the damn thing.

Just then a small lizard ran between Akando's feet, and Iye sprang from the man's arm and flashed off after it.

"Iye, no!" called out Akando.

The Lizard stopped in the shade beneath the machine; and the Falcon landed on one of the antennae.

Strong snorted. "So much for lightning bolts."

Akando reminded Kimama how the machine had not harmed the horses earlier.

"Huh." said Dan. "You think maybe it's just people, then?"

A whirling sound drew their attention back to the machine.

"Look!"

A cover was opening near Iye's perch. Then a four-inch mirrored cube poked out and rotated to face the falcon, which immediately spotted his reflection and pecked aggressively at it.

A fearful Akando jammed the whistle into his mouth and blew. "Iye, come!"

He blew harder. Dan, Strong and Kimama held their ears. Iye pecked. Akando whistled. The mirror vibrated. And all at once, the reflective cube disintegrated into thousands of tiny shards.

Iye yelped and flew at once to Akando. And a second later, an effulgent beam leaped from the ruptured opening. It was accompanied by a sound not unlike a frightened organ chord. And the machine went suddenly dead.

With a profound sense of awe, Akando whispered, "Iye has killed it."

Strong looked at Dan.

"If it really is dead, it won't hurt us, right?"

"Theoretically."

She drew her courage about her, extended a tentative finger out to touch the machine, which immediately on contact with her hand, dissolved in its entirety into a fine, silvery powder that mixed with the passing dust devils and flew away.

"Jesus, Mary and Joseph," murmured Strong, apparently convinced that the moment required a spiritual invocation.

Dan said, "Guess that answers the question about whether we'll be taking it with us."

Akando backed away a quick step. "We're not giving the money back."

"Forget that."

Just then the laser phone on Dan's belt beeped. Dan reacted with surprise, then keyed the device and brought it up to his ear.

"Yes?"

And a voice came back to him from hundreds of miles away. Clear as day, Joel Shank said, "Dan. Thank God. This is Joel Shank. The link's not gonna last more'n a few seconds."

Strong, Kimama and Akando gathered in a circle around Dan and his phone.

"Joel? Aren't you and Hans in Colorado?"

Ø

From the shadow of tall conifers, Joel Shank spoke into the phone at the opposite end of the signal that connected him to Dan and Alison Strong in the desert southwest.

By that time, he and Hans were inside the barbed wire of what he and Hans Odenwelder had earlier thought to be an abandoned hippie commune.

It had proved, in fact, to be a survivalist stronghold, commanded by one Jeremiah Magwood, who, along with several of his armed militiamen stood close by and listened.

Shank was trying to explain to Dan how the peaceful commune had turned out to be a base for something called the Freedom Strike Brigade.

In obvious response to a question from the other end, Shank said, "No, no, we're fine."

Magwood rested a beefy hand on Shank's shoulder.

"In fact, they wanna help us fight aliens. Hans figured out how to bounce our signal off passing satellites. If you connect with the other teams, tell them we're heading for -- hello. Hello?"

He looked at Odenwelder and the Militiamen.

"Gone."

Then as Shank clipped the phone back onto his belt, Magwood slapped him on the back, nearly knocking him over.

"Cheyenne Mountain," Magwood grinned. He offered an out-turned palm and Shank clumsily high-fived it.

Shank grinned back. "Yeah. Cheyenne Mountain."

Ø

Geographically quite far away, headed almost directly south from the militia compound, Dan pulled the phone from his ear and switched it into the standby mode.

"Lost him."

Strong turned to Kimama and Akando and asked, "How far would you say it is to Harper Lake?"

Kimama pointed across the hot sand.

"About a hundred miles."

Chapter 10
"Capitol Offenses"

Both geographically and politically distant from either Colorado or the great southwest desert expanses, only a quick walk south out of the Capitol rotunda, the United States House of Representatives was about to go into session.

For the first time in more than a hundred years, the proceedings were going to be conducted by the light from kerosene lamps.

When Frank Farrell, Tiffany Diamond and Ricky Escobar arrived on the scene, they found the chamber an only partially filled House, some of the elected representatives apparently unable to transport themselves from their home states to the capital.

Another striking anachronism soon surfaced. It had to do with Ricky's camera. Other reporters and photographers had been forced to fall back on still cameras or old-time crank movie cameras. They all crowded around Ricky and his functional video equipment. Their envy, often taking the form of downright hostility, became immediately apparent.

"That's the same camera I use. How come yours works and mine doesn't?"

All Ricky could do was shrug innocently. "Freak of nature, man."

"I'll give you ten grand for it."

"No way."

"Bet you can't say <u>no</u> to twenty-five."

"The camera's not for sale. Period."

"Thirty."

Just then a gavel sounded from the podium.

The Speaker had arrived and was ready to begin the business of the House.

"Ladies and gentlemen, we do finally have a quorum. All members will please take your seats. And the House will be in order."

A woman near the front stood up.

"Mister Speaker."

"Recognize the Honorable Ms Pellegrino."

"Thank you, Mister Speaker. Now that the Honorable Mister Farrell has arrived, I wonder if he might respond to persistent rumors he is at least tangentially linked to Mister Neil A Sepaca, the same Mister Sepaca who may bear some responsibility for our current dilemma?"

The Speaker watched Frank take his seat.

"Mister Farrell? Would you care to respond?"

Frank stood.

"Yes, Mister Speaker. First of all I would like to commend the Honorable Representative from the state of Nebraska for including all those qualifying words in her lead-in to be something of a non-question. There was the word rumors, which she described as persistent, a strange choice, perhaps, given that the crisis to which she makes reference only came to pass overnight. She refers to what she calls my tangential links, which she does not specify … and then she goes on to indict Mister Sepaca in the same indirect fashion."

Representative Pellegrino stood again. "I have not really heard an answer to my question."

"And," rejoined Frank, "I have not yet heard a question. Something more resembling a political stump speech to my ear. But as for exactly who might deserve some blame for this disaster, I would like to remind the House that it was the Emergency Preparedness Committee chaired by Ms Pellegrino that ignored the aforementioned Mister Sepaca's warnings of a coming crisis."

Pellegrino blustered again. "I would have hoped this would have been a time when we could have avoided partisan name calling and finger pointing. I would just like to get a straight answer from the

Honorable Mister Farrell. Does he or does he not know the present whereabouts of Mister Neil Sepaca?"

"I last had contact with Mister Sepaca a little over twelve hours ago."

"That still does not answer my question."

"Then your question will have to go unanswered."

The chamber erupted into a clamor of angry voices, which was not the least diminished by the Speaker's energetic gavel pounding.

In the commotion, Frank, Tiffany and Ricky exited the chamber.

Ø

Frank, Tiffany and Ricky emerged from the boisterous House chamber into the shadowy, nearly deserted Statuary Hall. Ricky kept his camera rolling.

Tiffany walked around in front of Frank, briefly blocking his progress.

"Well, that was certainly interesting."

He faked left, walked to the right, and got around her without breaking his stride.

"Never hurts to send them home guessing."

His eyes locked with Tiffany's.

They smiled.

Frank said to Ricky, "Could you shut the camera off for a sec?"

"Why?"

"Something I've been dying to do."

With that, Frank leaned toward Tiffany. She lifted her face. They kissed. After several seconds, Frank stepped back from her.

"We've got an appointment with the Senate Majority Leader."

She wiped lipstick off his mouth. And looking again into his eyes, raised her brows inquiringly.

"So you really don't know where Sepaca is?"

He shook his head.

"I can only imagine."

Chapter II
"Shadow Boxing"

Somewhere below, hundreds of feet beneath the innocently-fluffy belly of the camouflage cloud, there lay the vast expanses of open Atlantic Ocean water.

Sky Haven floated inside the swirl of moisture, both real and artificial, its three giant propellers sitting motionless.

All around the great dirigible small, gray orbs danced along beneath fat balloons.

Those orbs and the balloons held a special importance for Captain Stackhouse, crisply uniformed, gray at the temples, as he peered past the high-tech instrumentation and studied the thickening haze just outside the curved windscreen.

He turned to a crewman wearing a stethoscope listening device and softly inquired of the man a simple, "Well?"

The crewman listened then pointed in the direction of eight o'clock starboard.

What the crewman heard was out of sight, a mile, perhaps two, distant, as hidden by the haze as was Stackhouse's elegant craft.

Their number, that quartet of ACRONYM attack helicopters, remained unchanged as they churned into the edge of a cloud bank that extended uninterrupted for several miles in every direction.

Captain Jolly remained in command of the lead chopper. He squinted at the thickening soup outside, then glanced over at his copilot, who was holding a fat tube to one ear.

"Anything?" asked Jolly.

The copilot frowned and shook his head.

On the busy Sky Haven bridge, Stackhouse turned as his boss, Neil Sepaca entered the nerve center and moved up near to the captain

Stackhouse whispered, "Rotor sounds, closing, sir. We're running silent."

Sepaca nodded. "Do they know we're here?"

"More like a random search. But they're probably at least a little suspicious."

He turned to a crewman at another station.

"Activate the mine grid."

The crewman directed a laser at the closest floating orb, which responded by switching a light on its top into a flashing mode. That mine then relayed the beam to its nearest neighbor and so on, until all the balls were winking like holiday tree lights.

Stackhouse and Sepaca watched the audio crewman apprehensively.

The crewman nodded. "They're almost on us."

Stackhouse slapped a fat, red button on a nearby bulkhead. And inside a gunnery bubble two levels and half a ship away, a command light came on; the gunner, wearing protective gear, took the controls; and the transparent ball rotated, pointing its twin guns toward the approaching targets.

All around the dirigible other gun blisters twisted this way and that, like an athlete warming up, all training their muzzles on the same spot in the clouds.

Chapter 12
"Seen the Light?"

The hostile parties closed on one another. They were by that time engulfed in the same formation of clouds.

Jolly leaned forward inside the cockpit of his lead helicopter and squinted past the windshield wipers.

Suddenly he whispered urgently, "I see blinking lights."

And an instant later, the clouds ahead broke, revealing the enormous dirigible inside the clearing storm's eye.

"My God," gulped the copilot. "I had no idea it was this huge."

At that same moment, pinpoint muzzle flash broke out from gun blisters all along Sky Haven's skin. Searchlights swept the gloom.

As the fierce defensive fire from Sky Haven rattled around the helicopters, they formed an attack line and returned fire.

Bright tracer rounds laced the cloud's dark interior.

Inside the dirigible, a round whined out one wall of a companionway and through another, dropping a running crewman in mid-stride.

Jolly turned his lead helicopter for a direct assault.

The copilot ducked.

"Mine!"

Directly in front of them, a blinking globe bobbed up right in line with the windscreen.

The air went suddenly black. And Jolly's chopper shed parts, as it began a slow, twisting dive.

On that same side of the battle, flames spit suddenly out through two large holes in Sky Haven's side. And the behemoth tilted heavily in the directions of its wounds.

It seemed at first as though those fires alone were lighting the cloud bank's interior. But quite soon, those who were still able saw the beam, a sizzling thing, brighter than unfiltered sunlight, it refracted inside the dizzying haze, as it cut downward and enveloped both the dirigible and the remaining helicopters.

Within seconds, Sky Haven's fires seemed to have extinguished on their own; and the listing ship had completely righted itself.

Moreover the falling chopper had canceled out its own plummet earthward, actually stopped its fall in mid air, as if frozen inside clear, pure ice.

And a few seconds later, all four helicopters, even the one that had begun breaking apart, levitated toward the unseen source of the light, finally vanishing completely from sight.

No one, with the exception of Sepaca, had seen anything of what had happened. They had all cowered from the blazing light.

And during their blindness, without their being any the wiser, they had all flickered momentarily from view and returned several times, shed bright pixels and buzzed like swarms of angry hornets.

Only when the light finally went out for good, did all return to normal; and the members of the Bridge Crew were finally able to open their eyes again.

One of them, trembling from pure fright, turned wide eyes on Sepaca and asked, "What in God's name was that?"

Sepaca turned and headed for the hatchway.

From over his shoulder, his voice came back to them cool and reassuring.

"A gentle caution, most likely. Good work, Captain Stackhouse."

Stackhouse steadied his wobbly knees and made a business of smoothing his rumpled uniform.

"Thank you, sir." To the crew in general he commanded, "Get us moving." And as if it were an afterthought he added, "And deploy a dozen decoys."

He peered out through the transparency that made up the forward two-thirds of the bridge's superstructure.

At first the sky inside the cloud lay as empty as it had been before the battle. But very soon an elongated object cruised outward from beneath his vantage point. Another followed soon after that and another and nine others, each forming a camouflage cloud of its own, all of them following different headings as they slowly receded into the mists of a common uncertainty.

Stackhouse took a step backward that carried him outside of the command circle.

Still he lingered.

"Will you be in your quarters, Sir?" inquired his second in command.

"I will not."

The entire bridge crew turned to look at their captain.

"Then where will we find you, sir?"

"Just look over your shoulder. I'll be right there."

"Here, sir? You mean to remain on the bridge?"

"I have not yet been relieved of my command. Until then, Sky Lab remains my ship. Do not be fooled. The war has not been won. Even this first battle is far from over. It has barely begun."

Chapter 13
"Lowdown Hoedown"

Date palm fronds combed a taste of salt out of the gentle trade winds and made dancing shadows out of the noonday sunlight.

Only a few yards out from the shoreline sands, a pair of sails came down the mast on an ocean-going ketch. It had just then come to a bobbing anchor on the placid water that spread out inside a gap where two fingers of land nearly touched.

A skiff, rowed by a man with a woman passenger, set out from the ketch, passed through the narrow inlet, and slipped into a perfectly circular cove

The skiff came smoothly aground and Natalie Misaka and Paul Grigsby easily walked it up onto the sand.

Natalie cocked her head to one side and turned an ear in the direction of a musical sound, hardly of the Caribbean variety, more Blue Grass southern comfort.

Paul Grigsby heard it, too.

"A hoedown?"

"Even NASA retirees like to party, Paul."

They set off on foot to locate the source of the music.

Paul and Natalie soon came upon a sign that identified the locale as the Smart Set Retirement Community.

Up-scale, palm-shaded homes faced the cove and ocean beyond, across a public space, where gray-haired couples in western attire danced to fiddle music from a wind-up gramophone.

One man, standing atop a bale of hay, gave the calls.

"We got no lights, we got no power; but we can square dance, by the hour."

The dancers shuffled and promenaded with youthful vigor, seemingly oblivious to Misaka and Grigsby's tentative approach.

"Nothing's showing, on teevee; I've got arthritis in my knee."

As the phonograph lost RPMs, the caller hopped down off the hay bale and went to give it a crank. And that was when he spotted Misaka and Grigsby.

He never missed a beat in his call.

"Time we gave ourselves a rest. Especially since we've got some guests."

He lifted the tone arm off the record; and to Natalie and Paul he offered up a chirpy, "Howdy."

Chapter 14
"Gotcha"

Having just parted company with Akando and Kimama only minutes earlier, Dan and Alison Strong tried to retrace their back through the arroyo and then follow their rapidly-eroding foot prints in the sand back toward their landing site.

"I think it's back through that little pass up there, Dan'l," Strong told Dan.

And, indeed, when they finished the twists and turns along the gentle climb, they came between two rocky shoulders and looked down at their plane.

By that time, it had gained a companion, a black helicopter with an ACRONYM logo.

Strong hissed, "Down, Dan'l!"

They dropped prone and squinted through the small sand storm stirred up by the chopper's slowly turning blades.

"Looks abandoned," ventured Dan.

Strong was less certain.

"I don't like not seeing the crew."

A deep voice, not Dan's, said, "Right here, Sunshine."

Dan and Strong turned onto their backs and found three troopers aiming weapons down at them. The biggest among them, the one doing the talking, gestured with his rifle barrel.

"Now get up and move yourselves out there next to the chopper."

Ø

Following their brief and decidedly hostile first contact, the five of them had made a hasty descent out of the arroyo into the flying grit that spun around the plane and the helicopter.

Dan and Alison Strong had offered not the slightest resistance. The three automatic rifles and the determined faces behind them had provided all the encouragement they needed to do as their captors instructed.

The talking trooper said, "We saw you kill the generator."

He shoved Dan in through the open chopper door. One of the other troopers moved around the plane.

Strong hesitated before boarding the plane.

"Where're you taking us?"

"Gonna meet up with some friends."

He pushed Strong then into the seat next to Dan. The second trooper took the pilot's seat; and the third came at a run from Sepaca's plane, carrying the red box on his shoulder. As soon as he had boarded, the talking trooper yelled, "Take 'er up!"

The craft leaped at once into the air. And as it climbed quickly to an altitude of several hundred feet, Dan and Strong's plane exploded in a sphere of fire that careened and bounced like a crazed cue ball across the sand below them.

Chapter 15
"In A Tight Spot"

It was always dark in the pastureland hole there beneath the machine on the Burwell family's Amish farm.

Zipper did not really seem to mind the closeness of the walls or the damp, earthy smells, that no doubt included ample portions of cow dung.

But Fish, having once, as a child, been briefly trapped inside an abandoned refrigerator, which he had climbed into on his own, ignoring dire warnings of the likely consequents, hated confinement of any type.

"It's one reason I've even avoided marriage," he told Seth as they stood there side by side, watching the boys at work.

Even standing on open ground at a cautious distance from the machine, Fish felt the sweat running down his spine and pooling in his shorts.

Good job, he thought, that he had abandoned all pretense of machismo and left the digging to the youngsters.

They were, Zipper and Caleb, down there at the moment, crammed together into the tight space, all that was allowed by the narrow spread of the machine's tripod feet.

Seth leaned toward Fish and in a rather quiet voice said, "My own fear is about being someplace up high, especially with no railing."

Fish nodded. "See, everybody's just different, that's all. Heights don't really bother me at all."

Both men could clearly hear Zipper joking and jabbering to himself, offering prompts on what to do next as he and Caleb burrowed straight up.

"Getting close, Caleb, m'man. Better cover your eyes."

Fish knew that if he had been in that hole, there would have been scarcely enough air to fill his lungs, let alone carry on a real conversation, one that required some rational thought process.

"Ah," gurgled Zipper's voice, as the first fleck of grass root came down with the sod, an obvious suggestion that their shovels were finally cutting through to fresh air.

"Yikes!"

That was Caleb's voice as a shower of dirt, small stones, leaves and probably some ripe cow offering dropped over the two of them.

Fish gagged.

Seth looked at him.

"You all right, Mister Fishbourn?"

Fish covered his mouth and nodded.

Anyway, the boys were cheering.

"We're through, Dude. So far no killer ray beam."

The two of them poked their dirty heads up from a hole and grinned from beneath the metallic underbelly at Sara and Seth and, especially, Fish.

"Well, here goes nothing," yelped Zipper. And he reached up and touched the machine with a single tentative forefinger.

They all waited.

Nothing happened.

Zipper poked the machine.

"Hey ... hello ... anybody in there?"

Still nothing happened.

Fish, Seth and Sara cheered. Seth actually hugged Fish.

And then Seth turned to Sara and said, "Somehow, against my better judgment, I find myself warming to that boy."

She smiled. "Uhm ... me too."

"Spite of his peculiar ways, he's a whole lot better'n some of the others we've let in."

"I caught one stealing eggs this morning," she told him.
He shook his head.
"Not like we're letting anybody go hungry.
Fish waved to Caleb.
"We should switch places so I can help Zipper."
Caleb nodded, ducked down, and with rabbit-like speed, quickly wriggled his way to the escape hole.

Ø

As soon as he was clear of the pit outside the machine's zap zone, Fish took a couple of deep breaths and dropped down below the surface.

There was the tunnel, of course. But how hard could that be?

He went head first into it, telling himself it was just like getting born. Probably not a good comparison, on second thought. His memories of the delivery room were rather sketchy; but he was pretty sure the birth canal was not reinforced with salvaged lumber from some old barn.

The ceiling was low; and he was sweating profusely by the time he came up at the other end and had enough room to stand up beside Zipper and share the young man's awe by the nearness of the alien artifact.

He ran his hand over the smooth surface and shook his head. "Well, so far so good."

Zipper beamed.

"Hell of a thing, huh, Mister Fishbourn?"

"Indeed it is, Zipper. "Not forgetting that we've still got to crack into this damned thing."

"You're looking a little pale, man."

"Some minor claustrophobia. No biggie."

Together they dusted off the machine's underside and adjusted the reflector on a kerosene lamp so as to see more clearly.

Almost at once, Zipper pointed.

"What does that look like to you?"

Fish squints.

"A port of some kind?"

"Uh-huh. Do you think there's even the slightest chance that Mister Sepaca would send us this far with no way to tap into the machine?"

"Meaning, time to open the box?"

"Depends, Daddy, on whether you think it's really Christmas."

They grinned at one another.

Chapter 16
"Water Words"

Dark clouds scuttled across the sky. They moved fast, as if running from something genuinely worthy of fear.

A sign rattled in the wind. It read: "Padre Island Inter-Species Language Center".

Professor Farrell and Ursula Fontaine waded into the gentle surf of an inlet off the sea. They already saw beyond the headlands how the waves were increasing in frequency and size.

Each took a fish from a pail floating between them and sailed it out over the water.

And immediately two bottlenose dolphins appeared, leaped into the air, and caught the fish in their mouths. Then the Dolphins swam in close to the humans.

And they spoke most politely.

"Hello, human Farrell."

The second one greeted Ursula.

"Hello, human Fontaine."

Ursula asked them where they went whenever they disappeared from the inlet adjacent to the center.

Dolphin Two replied, "Secret for us."

"What about the aliens?" asked Farrell. "Were they a secret, too?"

"Yes," said Ursula. "How come you never told us?"

Quite matter-of-factly, Dolphin Two replied, "Not asking us."

"Friend whales sing songs on Star People since hundreds human years," volunteered Dolphin One. "But dolphins not believe them for long time. Whales such liars."

Farrell's phone beeped suddenly to life with Shank's broken voice coming hissy through from the other end.

"Hello? Anybody there?"

Farrell jumped, startled. He quickly keyed the phone.

"Joel. Is that you?"

Dolphin One demanded, "What human calls?"

"Friends," Ursula told him.

Ø

Inside the eggshell observatory dome, Louise Padget and Hollis Cryer ceased cranking the huge telescope into position and held their phone between them.

It was Dolphin One's voice that came through first, "Hello, Friend Humans."

Alvin Farrell's voice came back through the speaker. "How'd you do this?"

"Tell you later."

Louise Padget leaned forward and spoke into the radio.

"Padget and Cryer here, too. This is fantastic."

The scene back at Sandy Cove was near euphoric. The square dancers surrounding Natalie Misaka and Paul Grigsby applauded with unbridled enthusiasm.

Grigsby hushed them and said, "Paul Grigsby and I hear you loud and clear."

Shank's voice came back sharply, "Not likely to stay that way for very long, I'm afraid."

In fact, at that moment, Shank and Odenwelder were aboard a smoke-belching locomotive from the 1950's era, as it pulled half a dozen vintage cars across a trestle bridge.

The two of them, along with Commander Magwood and a pair of other militiamen occupied a dining coach, wherein some of the tables held coffee cups, dirty dishes and other remnants of a recent meal.

"I talked to Dan and Alison earlier," said Shank into the radio. "Just checking, Dan. Are you there? No? Well, Hans and I are on our way to —-"

Suddenly a series of ear-piercing crackles cut through the transmission; and a new voice slithered into the conversation.

It belonged to Ator Guinard.

"My thanks to all of you. Your chatter has made it so much easier for me to locate all of you."

Chapter 17
"Troop Ship"

On that moonless night, in all of Paris, only the Ile de la Cite showed even a trace of electric light.

There persisted, moreover, directly off the island's eastern tip, a most peculiar glow that stained the water and even an unusual fog that rose up from just that one spot.

Still, the real terror lay well out of sight, deep below the waterline, in a dusky chamber that was a part of Guinard's underground crypt.

The level floor of the space rose about five feet above a large, dark pool of lapping water.

All of that might have been strangely noteworthy, had it not been reduced to insignificance by a familiar shape at rest atop the elevated surface.

It was a thing both flat and thick, silvery, thrice blistered on its top.

Presently, Guinard entered the chamber by way of a crudely hewn archway cut through the bedrock. His cloak flapping behind him created an image of a man on the verge of actually taking flight.

Other biped forms raced to match his long stride.

They crossed the chamber floor in seconds, mounted the gentle incline and entered the humming disc.

Chapter 18
"Battle Gear"

The great machine vibrated slightly, even at its core, where an egg-shaped crew space held three dozen armed troopers, all waiting silently, strapped securely into a series of niches that completely surrounded the lower wall.

Just above them, a circular mezzanine contained the control area, whereupon two humanoid shadows huddled before liquid displays that rippled right and left, up and down across sculptured bulkheads.

Guinard turned his horned head to consider a holographic Earth globe, whereon several spots blink blue.

And he hissed in clear displeasure, "Except, or course, for you, Sepaca. Always the fox through the hole in any garden's wall."

Ø

Sepaca's eyes, showing no emotion as they flicked over the monitor where Guinard's image played.

"But even so wily an opponent as you, Sepaca, cannot evade me forever."

Sepaca pressed a button built into the desk.

"Captain Stackhouse, can you increase our velocity?"

Immediately, an almost-arterial beating raised its pace through the decking. Sky Haven was traveling at full speed.

Ø

The Seine bubbled all around the southern tip of the island; and from that point, the greenish glow separated itself from the bedrock and with gathering momentum, moved down river. Seconds later, the current abruptly parted somewhere in midstream and a silvery disk sprang into the air, dragging a sheet of boiling water and steam behind it.

The thing rose over the city and turned westward.

With the priest at his side on the control deck, Guinard turned from the controls and stepped into the light, where his scaled flesh shone and the horn in the middle of his forehead cast a long shadow across his face.

"In the meantime, it is comfort enough to hear the voice of my Oracle."

On a rue beneath their arching assent, horses pulling a coach shied at first sight of the hovering disk which, in the absence of the moon, was the brightest thing in the sky.

It rose steadily, shining through breaks in the clouds that shed light drizzle over the city.

The coach driver, fearful quiver in his voice, spoke to the horses. "Steady."

Very quickly, the disc moved noiselessly away; and the river's waters settled again into their natural, civil flow.

Chapter 19
"Basic Training"

The train belched a roil of black smoke from its stack and blew its whistle as it chugged from the mouth of a rock-rimmed tunnel.

Inside the dining coach, Magwood and his militiamen formed up in a smart half circle in front of Shank and Odenwelder.

The commander wiped one oversized hand across the dark stubble covering the lower half of his face; and he said quite calmly, "You can cast it in any light you want, boys. But this here is Armageddon."

To a man, the Militiamen cheered.

Magwood cleared a table with a sweep of his arm and rolled a map out flat for all to see.

"Once we get down here to Colorado Springs, there'll be a pack train and a guide waiting to take us on in."

Taking chance notice of Shank and Odenwelder's dour expressions, Magwood smiled. "Hey, don't look so bothered. We've been getting ready for this since 1972. Every time there's some kind of a disaster, those boys gather up the mules and the horses and wait for us at the trailhead, just in case we need 'em."

After a moment's reflection on his own, he added, "So far, we never have."

Nearby, the train's whistle sounded again.

Far away, beyond the chug and blast of the train, a bit away even from the shifting ambiguities of the desert, there lay the uncompromising certainty of a paved road.

Its permanence, freshly painted yellow stripe and all, cut through clumps of houses and a school, a fire station, and a community center.

It formed, collectively, the reservation where Kimama and Akando lived.

In an open field across the road from the school, two dozen sheep cowered from a ACRONYM chopper that broke the corn stalks down flat to the ground with its rotor wash.

The side doors crashed open and two dozen troopers bounded out and went loping over the blacktop toward the buildings.

In one house, an old woman and man lay in reclining chairs, snoring loudly. The door burst open; two troopers charged in, checked the side rooms and dashed out again.

The man and woman never noticed.

Two houses down, the front door hung from a single hinge. Troopers conducted a violent search that involved slapping a young mother, wailing babe in her arms, and punching her male companion into a stupor.

Then, in some unknown way satisfied, they departed that abode, as suddenly as they had come; and they moved on to the next building down the road, which was the schoolhouse.

It fared no better.

Kimama stood at the front of a class of grade scholars. She scribed chalk numbers on a wallboard, then turned and looked at all the bright faces focused on her.

"Two hundred seventy-two divided by eight." She read out to them. "Who knows the answer?"

The kids raised their hands. Kimama picked out a girl.

"Amitola."

The girl smiled broadly at having been chosen.

"Thirty-four." She piped proudly.

Kimama clapped her hands in appreciation.

"That's ri --"

With the rest of the word still stuck in her throat, her dark eyes went wide in alarm, as both the front and back doors came open simultaneously and the room filled with two squads of heavily-armed men.

Some amongst the children began to cry at once, as the troopers seized Kimama and dragged her toward the back of the room.

"Who are you?!" she cried. "Why are you doing this?!"

The troupe commander whacked the back of her head with his open hand.

"You work for the people who destroyed the machine, the one that came down in the desert!" he growled at her.

"No ... I just took them to it! Ow!"

"You were seen taking money from them."

One boy jumped up from his desk and tried to help Kimama. But the troopers knocked him to the floor, where he lay bleeding from his mouth.

Ø

The first thing Kimama saw as the troopers propelled her out of the school's front door was her own house burning.

"No!" she cried. "My things, my ancestors' pictures! Please let me save them!"

One particularly large trooper holding her left arm lifted her off the ground and shook her like a rag doll.

"Maybe you'd like to go join your ancestors, huh?"

From the opposite direction, there came another group that had taken Akando prisoner. He immediately saw Kimama's plight and struggled to reach her.

"Let her go! We haven't done anything!"

But the troopers ignored him. Their two forces merged; and in a single wave, they washed back across the road toward the helicopter waiting in the field, its rotors turning listlessly.

And just as they reach the landing zone, another chopper settled toward the field. It carried Dan, Alison Strong and the set of troopers who captured them.

They all looked down on the raiding party rushing along beneath them.

The trooper in charge of the just-arrived craft said to his pilot, "Take us down alongside."

And as his ship settled earthward, the raiding party dragged Kimama and Akando into the first chopper.

"Go!" their leader ordered.

The engine barked to life. The rotors chopped to life over their heads.

And just as they began to rise, a dark shape shot through the still open door. Akando's falcon landed on the pilot's headrest.

"Iye!" yelled Akando in clear surprise.

The Pilot swatted at the bird; and the falcon fought back beak and talon.

"Oh god! Get it off me!"

In that moment of wretchedly bad timing, the second chopper's landing gear was just then pressing into the corn and the commanding trooper had just begun to slide open the side door.

First Strong, then the others saw the raiding helicopter gyrating wildly in their direction.

Someone screamed, "Look out!"

Dan pushed Strong toward the door, which still stood partially ajar.

"Jump!"

Together, they dived out the door, their fall thankfully softened by the plowed earth.

As their heads came up, they saw the assault chopper bounce on the ground, and spotted Kimama and Akando, as they also leaped clear, stumbled, helped one another up again, and ran.

It seemed no one, no thing, could prevent the obvious. Both helicopters continued to rise. Their main rotors tangled. An instant later, the first craft turned on end and settled onto its tail. The other craft rolled onto its side, spun around several times in the dry dirt.

Then they exploded together in a single, blinding flash.

Ø

The burned helicopters retained their fatal embrace, side by side, partly in the field, partly blocking the road.

They continued to smoke and give up the occasional secondary bangs and pops, small, probably a stray piece of ordinance that survived the crash.

That was not the only thing still inside the wreckage of one of the parts of the burned and melted carcasses.

Dan managed to pull the red box out from underneath a twisted engine cowling. He hauled it over to where Strong, Kimama, Akando and the reservation residents, huddled in front of the school.

As he approached them, Alison Strong was saying in a soothing voice to Kimama, "Please tell the children how sorry we are for whatever part we played in this. It really was out of our control."

Kimama shook her head.

"Those men ... they destroyed themselves."

Dan joined them.

"Curious thing about that," he told them all. "There are no bodies."

Strong looked surprised.

"All burned up, then."

Dan held up the box.

"This wasn't even scratched."

As Akando cradled a slightly singed Iye in his arms, he asked Strong and Dan, "Will you still go to Harper Lake?"

"We have to," Dan told him.

"Do you ride horseback?"

Dan and strong both nodded.

"Yes."

Akando gazed again at the smoldering ruin in the cornfield.

"If I take you, will you tell me why they did this?"

Immediately Strong said, "Yes."

Dan added, "Better than that, we'll show you."

Akando turned to a man standing nearby.

"We'll need three saddle horses and a pack animal."

Kimama stepped out in front of them all and glared fiercely. "Make that four saddle horses." Then she added for Akando's ears only, "Not only do I ride better than you, I know a faster way to get there." And for Alison Strong's benefit, "He has a terrible sense of direction."

Then as she left them and walked off purposefully, Akando turned to Dan.

"In Shoshone the name Kimama means 'butterfly'. It should be 'wasp'."

He started after her.

Dan checked his watch then looked at Strong.

"Almost three days gone."

Chapter 20
"Disc Jockey"

Day's fiery ending ran blood red over the speeding disc, as it skimmed the Pacific's ocean waters so low that it and the sonic waves that chased it cut a narrow trough through the tallest of the waves.

On the bridge, Guinard activated a new set of overlays for the holographic globe. He seemed satisfied with the way in which the fresh projection showed many more of the red dots, which represented his forces, for every one of Sepaca's blue.

With no intent that his words might fall on others' ears, he told himself aloud, "Come morning, all will be ready."

The priest drifted up from the lower deck and asked, "How will you find Sepaca?"

Guinard actually laughed aloud for the first time. "Oh, I do not trust my powers to find him, Holy Man. I trust him to find me."

And as the disk rushed on, racing the sun into perpetual daylight, Guinard's voice took on an audible sneer.

"Such a fool, Sepaca, to place his trust in so frail and flawed a thing as humanity."

Chapter 21
"Prey or Play"

The large man in the dull gray suit and patriotic tie came with Frank, Tiffany and Ricky out a door that bore a sign that read: "SENATE MAJORITY LEADER".

The four of them paused in the murky corridor. The Speaker shook his head.

"Wish I had more time, Frank. But I have to attend a prayer dinner."

Frank thought to himself what a bloated fool the man was.

"Think maybe a little more action and less praying might be the wiser choice, Mister Majority Leader?"

The Speaker smiled and nodded.

"Oh sure. That would be my choice, too. But in times like this, the electorate likes to see their leaders chastened and on their knees in search of wisdom from on high."

"So instead of leading, you follow the sheep."

"Frank."

"Just get me into the White House."

The Speaker began to herd them along.

"Wouldn't help, Frank. The Secret Service's got the president locked down out at Camp David."

He pointed at Ricky and his camera.

"Can you make him shut that damn thing off?"

"'Fraid not, Mister Speaker."

"Hey, then I'm outta here."

He pivoted then with surprising agility and headed for a stairwell door, with Frank following part way.

"Sure you folks can find your way out," said the Speaker, as the door banged shut behind him.

Frank walked back toward Tiffany and Ricky. She smiled and grabbed Frank's hand.

"Come on."

Frank pulled his what-the-hell-are-you-talking-about face. "Where're we going?"

"You heard the man. The President's at Camp David."

Then, as the three of them headed off down the corridor together, Ricky wondered aloud, "How come you don't ever hold my hand, Frank?"

"Fear of rejection, Ricky."

... part three

*"The gathering winds
will call the darkness soon,
And profoundest midnight shroud
the serene lights of heaven."*
Percy Bysshe Shelly

Chapter I
"City Lightweights"

As day on the Burwell farm lost its color, Fish and Zipper lugged the red box between them toward the meadow excavation and their appointment with the machine that straddled it.

Along the way, purely by necessity, they passed through a growing encampment of folk from the nearby cities, whom the Burwells had admitted onto their land out of generosity and Christian kindness for those in dire need.

Several wood burning cooking fires had long since created the tiny settlement's own layer of smog that mainly hugged the immediate area around the encampment over to and including the well, just short of the Burwell's own residence.

All manner of make-shift shelters lined the way, some actual tents the occupants, in anticipation of their eventual need had somehow managed to transport from the city into the proximate countryside.

For those less prescient, crates and cardboard cartons and dirty tarpaulins made do as well.

Fish wrinkled his nose.

"Do you notice how much it stinks here, after just such a short time?"

"Pretty hard to miss it," agreed Zipper. "And not all that surprising, given the lack of facilities, wouldn't you say?"

Just then, a man ran at full speed out from between two of the shelters and nearly knocked Fish and Zipper off their feet.

"Hey!"

"Jeez!"

Quite soon, the importance of is hurry became evident, as a second man, a fourth again the size of the first, flung himself out from between the same two shelters, apparently in determined pursuit of the first.

"Out of the way, assholes!"

He paused long enough to spot his quarry amongst the sizable crowd of milling squatters in the common space. Then, having identified the man, raced after him.

"Come back here you son-of-a-bitch," he screeched in a surprisingly high and loud voice. His panting rage slowly faded into the near distance, as he continued on his pursuit. "I brought that water up from the well for my family, not for you to steal!"

The first runner might actually have escaped, had he not stumbled over something not seen in the dirt and landed flat on his face.

The fellow in pursuit was on him in a flash, which put him there only seconds ahead of Seth's arrival on the scene.

"Hey, hey, none of that or I'll have to ask you both to leave."

"I didn't steal his water or anything else."

"He did!"

"Can you identify it?" demanded the man on the ground.

"Huh?"

"Was it wet, maybe?"

"You little squash bug!"

Seth squeezed himself into the narrow danger zone between them.

"I said you two either have to stop it, or I'll put you both out on the road again."

The big guy seemed to be taking Seth's measure; and Seth was canny enough to know it.

"Never mind that," Seth told him. "I've wrestled bales of hay that weighed more than you do; so don't think you'd be too much for me to handle."

Seeing how the two men continued to glare at one another prompted Seth to add, "And I won't tolerate any more trouble out of either one of you, understood?"

They continued to glare.

"I asked if you understood."

The big guy said, "Yeah."

The smaller one said, "Yes sir, Mister Burwell, I fully understand the conditions of my continued stay on your property."

The big guy scratched his head.

"You're a lawyer, aren't you?"

"How'd you guess?"

Seth pointed north and south.

"You two go in opposite directions and stay clear of each other for however long you have to stay here."

Each with a final posturing glower did as he was told.

"Good work there, Mister Burwell," called out Zipper. "I admire your style, firm-but-peaceful."

Seth sighed as if about to fold under an uncommon weight.

"I do sometimes let my temper get the best of me; but there does have to be some form of order, even in the absence of real, official law."

Fish agreed. "And it didn't really seem to me like you overreacted."

Seth fell into step with the two of them, as they resumed their course toward the meadow.

And in that mode, they very soon reached the point where Seth and Caleb had lowered the wire fence so as to make Zipper and Fish's peregrinations to and from the site as convenient as possible

There was still noise, lots of it, reaching them from the camp. And as a result, Seth clearly remained an unhappy man.

"Hooligans," he grumped, as he watched the two men tote the red metal box into the thigh-high meadow grass.

"That bunch brought in a supply of alcohol with them and have since clearly indulged themselves to an excess."

"Uhm," sounded Zipper. "I'd be thinking they're probably trying to forget what's going on in the outside world."

"Dead wrong approach. God expects us to act in our own best interests." He gestures at them with both hands. "You two gentlemen may not share our beliefs; but you have never in the least insulted them nor taken our hospitality for granted."

"I wouldn't ever do that," gasped Zipper in clear dismay.

"Of course you would not. And that is because you are a good man and you appreciate that you are welcome on our land."

He looked at Fish.

"You're a little stuffy, but not so bad yourself."

"Thanks heaps," rejoined Fish flatly and nodded his head toward the source of the ruckus. "What will you do about them?"

"Tell them to get rid of the whiskey."

"They won't."

"Then they will have to go."

Fished squared himself. "If you need any help."

"Thank you."

"Oh, I was offering you Zipper. I'm a devout coward."

Seth studied them briefly. Then his face softened; he smiled thinly and actually tapped Fish on the chest with his forefinger.

"Who knows. I may decide you are a good man as well."

Fish bowed his head slightly.

"I am humbled."

Seth chuckled. "But not very much in that direction, I think."

He looked toward the rowdies, visibly thought the situation through for likely the hundredth time, then shrugged and walked off the way he had just come.

"If you fellas need help, I'll be up at the house."

Fish watched Seth go, then turned and found Zipper grinning at him.

"What?"

"Better watch it, or you'll end up mellowing out."

Fish narrowed his eyes. "Not likely as long as you're anyplace in the vicinity. Let's go."

They stepped in tandem then through the fence opening and picked up their pace along a clear trail of recently trampled grass.

Ø

"Admit it," demanded Zipper, as they approached the pile of dirt that topped the near horizon. "You're starting to fall victim to my inherent animal charisma, aren't you?"

Fish actually stopped cold and stared at Zipper.

"I'd rather pour hot lead down my shorts."

Zipper's face lit up.

"Hey, cool. I did that one time."

Fish blinked several times then laughed out loud; and they started to walk again.

"You are definitely a pervert."

"Thanks."

By that time, they had arrived at the hole that led down to the tunnel beneath the Machine.

They lowered the box into the pit, then dropped down after it.

Ø

During his absence from it, Fish had not learned to like the tunnel with its two-by-four roof supports any more than he had before.

He and Zipper pushed the box through the tunnel and brought it up under the machine.

Zipper watched Fish gasp in fresh air.

"It might take a little longer, man; but if it helps, I can do this thing by myself."

"No. No way on earth would I let you have that kind of leverage over me."

"I wouldn't."

"Let's just do the job and get the hell outta here."

"Okay," said Zipper. He rubbed off more dirt from the machine's bottom.

"If this doesn't work, I'm telling everybody it's your fault."

"It better work," Fish short back. He took another deep breath. "In which case, I'll take all the credit."

Zipper slid the box toward Fish.

"You first."

Fish hesitated, then cautiously touched a pad on the box; and a red beam leaped to his eye.

Zipper did the same thing, with like results.

They waited a second, then two.

"Why isn't it working?" demanded Zipper.

Then, finally something did click sharply internally, next to one of the red metal sides. And completely on its own, the lid slowly yawned wide, let out a faint gassy hiss and revealed a mint-green glow that filled the interior.

Zipper promptly dipped his hand into the box, felt about briefly, then pulled out the "chocolate bar" wired to a four-inch cube with multi-colored buttons all round.

As the cube cleared the box, the lights that encrusted it blinked to life.

Fish licked his lips.

"Sky Haven or no Sky Haven, Sepaca didn't invent that."

"For sure."

Then Zipper tapped a control on his wristwatch.

"Twenty-four hours till the power runs out."

As if sensing some urgency in Zipper's voice, Fish unreeled a second cable from the box and compared the connector at its end to the port on the machine.

Then he slipped the male jack into the female. There came another click from inside the machine, followed by a fainter one. And a part of the machine's underbelly split and opened downward to show an active display in perfect three dimensions.

Fish said, "Wow."

Without a sound, Zipper poked the display; and his finger went straight through it.

"Dude."

"Projection. The cube's the key pad."

"Let's see …"

Zipper worked the virtual keys. And with each stroke, the Machine drew intersecting grids out to infinity.

Visibly, a faint understanding ascended from the collar of Zipper's tee-shirt, up over face.

"Mister Fishbourn?"

"You wouldn't be addressing me, would you?"

"I need you to go with me on this."

Zipper's uncharacteristic sobriety brought bumps up on Fish's arms.

"What? Are we already screwed?"

Zipper raised his hand.

"Think. The display and the controls are all three dimensional, right?"

"Uh-huh."

"So the operating system, if you want to call it that, might be…"

Fish paled.

"Holy crap. You think they've added time?"

Zipper bit on his lower lip and nodded.

"Four dimensional."

Fish wheezed and felt the walls closing in on him.

"Can we even run it?"

Zipper's eyes darted back and forth.

"Good question. Are they using time like we do depth and width?"

"And if they are, is it linear time?"

"Yeah. Oh … whoa."

The Cube was beginning to sprout another projection with keys all its own. Another soon joined it, followed by two more. And their appearance left a hole in the center, wherein a tiny galaxy spun around a distinct black hole at its heart.

"Mister Fishbourn?"

"Do it."

With that, Zipper stuck his right index finger into the gap, let the galaxy swirl around its tip. He gasped.

"Zipper?"

"Oh … I see it now."

After another moment, with obvious reluctance, Zipper withdrew the finger and grinned at Fish.

"It's an icon."

"Icon?"

"Yeah," snorted Zipper through a thrilled laugh. "For a freaking operating manual."

Then he closed the Cube and worked his fingers around all four sides at the same time.

The display on the Machine whirled back and forth, sometimes leaping clear out of its frame and swirling around them both before diving back in again.

Finally Zipper relaxed and rested the Cube back inside the box.

And very calmly, he turned to Fish and said, "It's started."
"You got in?"
Zipper nodded slowly. He was pale and uncommonly subdued.
"When the germ evolves, the machine will send it up the control beam and infect the whole system."
A voice, sweet, soprano, reached them.
"Zipper? Mister Fish?"
Together, they peer out from under the machine and find Sara standing beside the hole, holding a lamp over her head.
Zipper managed a casual, "Hi."
Fish was surprised at the dusk and the lamp. He asked Sara, "How long have we been down in this hole?"
She seemed puzzled.
"You left the house five hours ago. If you're hungry, Ma's made supper."
Zipper slapped Fish on the back.
"Suddenly I'm starving."
Fish looks at him in disbelief.
"You're saying we can just leave it?"
Zipper had already disappeared into the tunnel. His voice came back. "It'll be fine."
He squirmed through the tunnel and climbed out of the hole. Fish followed close behind.
"What's on the menu?" Zipper asked Sara.
"Fried chicken, mashed potatoes and gravy, biscuits, green beans and apple pie."
He grasped her hand and said, "You're very beautiful."
She withdrew her hand shyly.
"Thank you," she replied, then added in soft rebuke; "But I should tell you that Amish boys do not court in such a forward fashion; and they nearly always do it through one of their male friends."
"Really?" Zipper pointed at Fish, freshly emerged from the hole. "You mean I have to date you through *him*?"
The two of them laughed together.
Sensing the joke had something to do with him, Fish said, "What?"

Chapter 2
"Family Values"

The night lay coldly black and pasted flat up against the outside of the kitchen window. In turn, the glass reflected back the light from three kerosene lamps stationed about the room as dependable agents of warmth in even those most uncertain of times.

While Miriam Burwell removed the last of the supper dishes from the table, Sara set plates with pie before her father, her brother and the family's two guests.

As she served Zipper, they exchanged smiles.

Caleb was complaining again; though no one seemed to be paying him much attention.

"Some Amish families let their kids have friends from outside and try out things from other cultures, but not in this house."

"It's called 'rumm-shpringa'," Sara translated for Zipper's benefit. "It means to 'run around'."

Seth made a disgusting smack of his lips.

"Boy thinks he's going off to New York City to act on the stage."

He turned to look specifically at Fish. "Are you a religious man, Mr. Fishbourn?"

"I'm what people call a 'cultural Jew', Mister Burwell. I can't really see myself ever entering a temple again."

Seth's head rocked back just a bit. He seemed to be acknowledging Fish's right to do whatever best suited his personal needs.

But the steadiness of his eyes bespoke a profound regret that Fish's choosing had so totally estranged him from his faith.

"Was it that God did something terrible to disappoint you?" he asked in a level voice.

"No."

"Might I ask, without prying too deeply, what it was, then?"

"It was the people who claimed they owned God. They were the real disappointment."

With that, Seth let his head rock forward again, as if finishing the nod of understanding he had begun seconds earlier.

"Might at least a few times in my life have shared that feeling. But it might also be a mistake, Mister Fish, to let other people control your relationship with God. That's something you should probably work out for yourself."

Fish's eyes drifted a bit.

"Your thinking being, then, that God is big enough to accommodate everybody?"

"Pretty much."

Fish turned a devious grin on Zipper.

"Even Zipper? Go ahead, Dude, tell the man what you are."

Zipper swallowed the last of his pie and, quite matter-of-factly said, "I suppose I'm pretty much a Hindu-Scientologist."

Seth wondered if Zipper was devout.

"Uhm ... oh ... I guess so, in my own way."

Miriam paused beside Zipper.

"I apologize if I'm being rude, Mister Zipper. But I've been studying the tattoos on your arms; and I was wondering if you'd mind talking about them."

Zipper smiled with delight.

"Oh, my skin art? Happy to tell you what all I know about it. They're actually pictographs from a variety of cultures around the world and throughout history."

He pointed to one.

"This right here you might recognize as the Cross of Saint John. This is an Ankh, an Egyptian symbol of life. I had these two copied off a frieze in a Mayan temple. This string of chicken scratchings is an old form of writing called cuneiform."

He singled out one last pictograph, which obviously represented a clock face.

"This one I don't really know about. As far as I know, it's always been there, since my earliest memories."

Seth had been studying the tattoos as well; and with a slight nervous edge to his voice, he said, "Well, guess it doesn't really matter much, so long as none of it's pagan."

"Not the way I look at it, sir. I just like the idea that people have always been looking for something bigger and more important than themselves. And these animal signs here are Hopi Indian. They celebrate the wonders of this great world that we human beings and all the other creatures live in."

"I see."

"I sincerely hope nothing about that offends you, Mister Burwell."

"And you say you are devout."

"Yes sir, I guess I am, pretty much so. Nonviolent."

There followed a peaceful silence totally absent of pressure, during which they all seemed to be trying to find some easy balance amongst themselves.

Finally Seth said, "Hasn't gone unnoticed how you've been making eyes at my daughter."

Sara's jaw dropped.

"Pa."

"Hush now."

Zipper's eyes met Seth's evenly and with barely a blink.

"Yes sir."

Seth regarded Zipper much like he might have a horse up for sale.

"Nothing. Just wanted you to know I took notice."

Miriam instinctively knew what the moment required. She stepped between Seth and Zipper and inquired of the tattooed young man and culturally Jewish Fish, "Would you boys like more pie?"

Zipper slid his plate in her direction.

"Yes ma'am, I surely would."

She filled the order immediately.

Fish patted his distended stomach and gracefully declined.

That business attended, Seth stood up.

"Well … days start early around here."

As he strode from the room, Caleb also got up; and he said very simply to Zipper and Fish, "I write songs, too".

He followed his father from the room.

Miriam respectfully let the silence hang for a moment, then she turned to Zipper and Fish and said, "You'll be cozy in the parlor tonight."

Fish thanked her for her hospitality.

Zipper stood as she left the room.

"Good night, Mrs. Burwell."

Chapter 3
"Night Deeds"

The darkness had a spongy thickness about it; and it hugged the ground almost conspiratorially.

Even the city slickers, the drinkers included, had long since packed it in or passed out for the evening.

All the lights on the ground floor of the main house were long out; and the last glimmer through an upstairs window soon vanished as well.

A comforting stillness settled.

There was, briefly, a dog bark, just twice.

That perhaps came in challenge to the slip and slide of a small shadow that cut itself loose from the weighty umbra skirting the house. It stole on two legs, the shadow did, across the farmyard, past the barn and through the break in the wire fence.

Once clear of the proximate farmyard, the figure moved openly, descending the last hillock to the hole beside the whirring machine.

It paused, apparently unaware that it was being observed from the tall grass nearby, where the tufted-eared wildcat lay flat, the animal's huge yellow eyes, long adapted to the night hunt, watching as the shadow looked all around and then lowered itself into the excavation.

The feline rose slowly onto its four feet and quickly vanished into the black.

Chapter 4
"Everybody Counts"

"You'll be in seven teams," said Natalie Misaka, "one for each of the Keplerian orbital elements."

Even as she saw the retired NASA residents there at the Sandy Cove Smart Set complex nod their understanding back at her, Natalie felt a genuine sense of the unreal about what it was they, along with her and Paul Grigsby, were about to do, or at least what they had every intention of attempting to do.

A dignified gentleman in the front row raised his hand.

"Just wondering how fast you expect to be needing these numbers."

Paul told him, "It could be only a few minutes after we get the final word."

A woman wearing a gaudy Hawaiian shirt and standing directly behind the dignified man reacted with clear surprise.

"We'll be doing this without computer support?"

Grigsby admitted that part remained a little iffy.

Natalie added, "We are working on that aspect of the project."

A man standing so close to Natalie that she could see him squishing sand between his bare toes piped up, "All modesty aside, Paul, Natalie, you've got some of the best scientific minds in the world here. And that would include the two of you."

The woman from before agreed. "But complex orbital numbers."

And the dignified man backed her up. "In the space of just a few minutes."

"Without a functional computer," added another voice from the back of the crowd.

Which prompted a small joke from the woman in the Hawaiian shirt. "Unless you're carting one around in that little red box of yours."

Most of them laughed at that idea.

Paul and Natalie did not. They seemed uncertain.

Still, the dignified man thought it was possible.

"Have to say my own brain isn't so fast as it might once have been. But we can back one another up, double check, all that."

Slowly the others nodded their agreement.

"With the right organization," someone offered.

"Right. Proper organization. That's the key."

Strangely, those few words seemed to satisfy all their qualms. In fact, a few of them had already begun to drift away from the larger group.

The Hawaiian-shirt woman asked Natalie and Paul, "Do you play shuffleboard?"

Paul and Natalie agreed in unison that they did not, a revelation that obviously disappointed the woman.

"Too bad. It's quite Newtonian, actually. Body at rest, body in motion, equal and opposite reactions."

With that she left them to join the bulk of the group, which had adjourned to a nearby shuffleboard court.

As she watched them choosing partners, Natalie's forehead organized itself into worried furrows.

Without looking directly at Paul, she asked, "Do you think they're right about the computer?"

He also remained focused on the shuffleboard court.

"'Bout it being inside the box?"

"Think maybe?"

"Best guess? If there is a computer in that box, we wouldn't need these guys."

They looked at one another, then made a cursory inventory of their surroundings.

Paul said, "Well, if it isn't especially the people, then there must be something important about this place."

They shaded their eyes and made an inventory as they scanned their proximate area.

"Sand and water," mumbled Paul. "That's all I see."

"Sunshine," added Natalie.

"Coral. Palm trees."

Natalie caught her breath.

"Coral?"

They turned to face one another.

Paul whispered, "It's a living thing."

In near synchronicity, they turned to look at the circular cove.

Again Paul spoke in a whisper, "A perfectly round body of water."

They hoisted the red box yet again between then and carried it to the water's edge.

Natalie smiled, as if partly in response to some fine, secret joke and ventured, "It fairly screams 'Sepaca'."

They paused there, toes only inches from the lap of tiny waves.

Paul chewed his lower lip.

"So … what if that's not it?"

She rested a hand lightly on his shoulder.

"Then we'll still have twenty-four hours to get it right."

He let out a long breath, as if to release the last of his uncertainty.

Then they squatted on either side of the box and concentrated so intently on it they failed to notice that the shuffle-boarders had left their game and formed a half circle behind them.

Natalie simply said, "Okay."

She rubbed her hands together quite vigorously, then tilted the box and pressed the trigger. Right away, the scan beam hit her eye.

The Smart Setters murmured amazement.

Paul followed Natalie's lead; and in seconds, the box lay open.

Behind them, the Smart Setters were straining to follow the action.

Natalie reached into the minty hazed interior and pulled out a pair of REX frames. Paul found a pair for himself, and together they slipped them on.

The lasers danced over their retinae, drew a convincing animation of the cove, even including the skiff positioned to plug the narrow opening out to the Atlantic.

From a red box like theirs, a man and woman withdrew a package that opened into a circular metal mesh, which they threw into the cove. The mesh expanded at once to fit the cove's contours. Then it sank and the animation followed it underwater. And as the mesh settled over the coral covering the cove's floor, ampules released microscopic organisms that formed chains between the coral stalks.

Back on dry land, the animated man and woman connected the mesh to the chocolate bar, then attached other lines to seven MINDMELD skull caps, which fit the heads of seven more human shapes.

The animation then went on board the VentureStar shuttle, where a man and woman who obviously represented Alison Strong and Dan responded to data fed to them from the coral computer.

The lasers went dead inside the REX frames. Paul and Natalie removed them and, for the first time, realize that the Smart Set residents had assembled themselves closely around them.

Natalie looked at Paul.

"Let's do it."

"Better'n shuffleboard," said someone behind them.

Chapter 5
"Camp David and Goliath"

All that afternoon, clouds, most of them broody and full of threat, had seemed determined to intercept the hot air balloon as it headed northwest out of D.C. and made a beeline for Camp David.

But the pilot and crew had caught a friendly tailwind rotating off the backside of a speedy line of storm cells; and it had scooted them to their destination just ahead of all the flash and roar.

The gondola carrying the pilot, Goggles and his passengers, Tiffany, Frank and Ricky, skimmed the tops of a thick oak and poplar forest, paused motionless for several seconds, and settled finally toward a vacant tennis court.

They had arrived just in time.

During their final descent, the advanced elements of the front rolled in for earnest and pulled the sky down with it. Fat raindrops began splattering all over on the gas-filled envelope and the gondola.

Tiffany pulled the hood of her jacket up over her head.

Goggles eased back on the burners. And it was he, looking over the gondola's edge to calculate their rate of descent, who first spotted the attention they had drawn.

"We've been detected," he announced quite simply.

The other three passengers peered down and watched as at least a half dozen figures, doubtlessly Secret Service agents, swarmed onto the tennis court.

An amplified voice called up to them, "This is a restricted area. You cannot land here. You cannot land here."

Goggles yelled back down, "I'm afraid we're not landing. We're <u>crashing</u>."

Tiffany glanced apprehensively over at Frank. He smiled back.

"I hate to lie," Goggles confided to his passengers with abject earnestness. "But it really is too late to climb back out of here."

There came almost at once a scrape from beneath their feet as the gondola touched down.

"Jeez!" Ricky sputtered in an alarmed voice.

They bounced twice lightly; and finally the gondola entangled itself on a fence and came to an abrupt stop.

Immediately the men on the ground swarmed all over it.

"Out! Out! Hands in sight! Hands in sight! Move it! Move it!" yelled the agent in charge, who seemed to think that saying everything twice doubled its impact.

In fact, that strategy seemed to work. Frank, Tiffany, Ricky and Goggles made a hasty exit from the gondola, Ricky hugging his camera to his chest, Frank the red box, both of which the agents roughly yanked from their grasps.

The agent yelled again, "On the ground! Now! Now!"

Chapter 6
"A Survivor's Song"

Perhaps fifty feet from the observatory wall, rooted atop a slight rise, a giant saguaro cactus stood, its prickly arms raised in perpetual surrender against the last of sunlight and the rise of the moon.

Nearby a low campfire flickered and popped within a circle of rocks. Its light cast animated shadows of the two humans, Louise Padget and Hollis Cryer, on the white dome.

Cryer took a skewer of meat from over the flames and offered Louise some. She took it reluctantly and tasted it with caution.

"Hmmm?" wondered Cryer. "I told you it tastes like chicken."

"Last time I checked, chickens had legs."

"Snakes are cleaner."

A coyote's howl turned Louise's eyes toward the darkness beyond the firelight.

"He's pretty far away, Cryer assured her.

She chewed.

"Coyotes don't scare me. Actually, it's kind of reassuring, something primal that says we've been this way before and everything's gonna turn out all right."

In the silence that followed between then, Cryer's eyes drifted away into some private musing. And he seemed faintly surprised when he hear his own voice asking Louise, "Does that mean you're tempted not to open the box so things'll just stay how they are now?"

Her slowness to answer might have meant she had given the idea some serious thought.

But instead she turned the question back on him.

"Are you?"

"Uhm ... been thinking it might not be all that bad."

She leaned in toward the fire.

"The snake isn't all that bad."

She tugged another chunk off the spit.

"You didn't really answer the question," he prompted.

She bit, chewed, took her time.

"Well ... been thinking about it." She bit again. Chewed.

"Of course, being out here, it's easy to forget how, in other places, the world's going to pieces right now."

He nodded and looked up at the sky. And he exhaled a reluctant sigh.

"Wouldn't be fair."

Louise sat very still and replied in a quiet voice.

"Guess not."

Chapter 7
"Too Many Players"

Commander Magwood's Militiamen, in the company of Shank and Odenwelder, lay on their bellies and took turns squinting through field glasses at a blocky structure built into the mountain's face.

A three-quarter moon provided only marginal detail and inky shadows.

The glasses made their way around again to Magwood; he looked, then said to the man beside him, "Collins, take Spivey and Furman and see what can you mouse out."

The man's masked head nodded understanding; and he and the other two selected troopers slipped away noiselessly, disappearing almost at once into the night.

"I couldn't see anybody," Odenwelder told Magwood.

"I don't have to see 'em," Magwood rumbled near Odenwelder's ear. "They're there, hunkered down. Waiting".

There was a touch of alarm to Shank's voice when he wheezed, "They knew we were coming?"

Magwood made a spitting sound. "Had to figure somebody like us would come, sooner or later."

"Whoa," breathed Odenwelder. "You saying there's others out here and they've got similar intentions?"

"It would surprise me if there wasn't"

As if to confirm his suspicions, muzzle flashes suddenly flailed out through the darkness and flares arched their way up from the building against the mountain and seemed to cling to the lower sky.

"Cover fire," barked Magwood.

His men opened up an impressive barrage of small arms fire that rattled off stone and metal somewhere down the slope.

And then the shadows below offered up a withering barrage of incoming fire that, despite the absence of muzzle flashes, certainly came from the areas around the building facade they had just been scanning.

"Down!"

Hot sparks spun spectacular firefly formations around the boulders that provided Magwood's force its cover.

Soon other flares launched from the rear of Magwood's position and off to his right flank. And gunfire rattled from all sides.

And less than a minute into the firefight, a light rush of air floated to them beneath the weapons chatter.

It sounded to Shank as if the night were breathing; and he was about to say just that, when a noisy wind washed over them. And through the flare light, a black helicopter dropped into the valley of their fighting; and it orbited; and it pumped rapid gunfire down on Magwood's troops.

Squeezed and twisted by the roar and screaming, Magwood's voice fell uncommonly small.

"Fall back!"

They zig-zagged through the boulder field that had made their fortress. And still the firing from the rear continued, even after the militiamen had retreated well out of range.

They paused, gasping, terrified and exhausted, long enough for Magwood to do a head count.

"Everybody here? Good."

His eyes found Shank and Odenwelder in the darkness.

"Aliens use ray guns, right?"

Shank, struggling to catch his breath said, "What're you saying?"

"Those boys behind us weren't Federales."

Odenwelder leaned into the exchange. "Another militia maybe?"

"Shit!" came Magwood's voice back at him. "Every gun's got its own sound. This was something like I never heard before. And that chopper."

Shank slumped to rest on a boulder.

"So how're we supposed to get in?"

There was still shooting in the near distance.

Magwood cleared his throat nervously.

"Requires a change of plans."

"No." Odenwelder's voice carried real terror with it. "We cannot do that."

"Flexibility, my little Nazi friend."

"Please, don't call me that. Being black and growing up in Germany has really made me nervous about such labels."

"Sorry ... courage, then."

One of his arms, barely visible to the unaided eye, pointed toward a sawtooth mountain range.

"There's an old Nike base over there. Five miles. It's mothballed, missiles're gone, but rumor has it the radar gear's still there. Deserted."

Odenwelder and Shank look for one another's shapes; and it was Odenwelder who gave voice to their common fear.

"But we do not know if our equipment will work in such a place."

Shank agreed at once. "Commander Magwood. You do understand what happens if we fail."

Magwood answered at once.

"All we can do is promise to get you boys in. Rest is up to you."

Chapter 8
"Fish Tales"

Waves lashed a glistening foam over the rocks around the pilings that held up the pier complex. The stiffening wind made a dull gray froth of the water and filled the air for miles with a constant spray that rose into the sky, up to where an almost straight black line marked a viscous churn of dark clouds that pressed down from unseen currents at work in the troposphere.

Some hours earlier, neither of those forces had yet assumed their full command of heaven and earth.

Now the palm trees had begun their surrender to the determined gale. And in only the past few seconds, a serious rain had moved into the inlet and begun to pepper the spot where two Dolphins waited half exposed in the water.

Professor Farrell and Ursula Fontaine struggled with umbrellas as they approached the shoreline from the direction of a nearby creaky metal building, the windows of which were already shuttered with plywood and two-by-four struts.

As the humans approached, Dolphin One piped, "Storm comes."

Fontaine nearly lost her footing on slippery rocks.

"It looks bad," she agreed.

"You call hurricane," offered Dolphin Two. "Feel pressure down."

Lightning cracked the near horizon.

"That's just great," moaned Farrell.

"Not great," Dolphin Two corrected.

"Danger!" agreed Dolphin One sharply.

Dolphin Two swam a quick circle around her partner and seemed to be appraising the sky.

"You go. Safe."

"Damn!" snapped Farrell.

"What wrong?" asked one of the dolphins.

"We can't leave," answered Ursula.

"House fall," piped Dolphin One. "Hurt human."

"If we go," Ursula told them, "other humans will be hurt."

"For good of pod?" asked Dolphin Two.

"Yes, for the pod," agreed Ursula.

Farrell looked at Ursula, his face gone slack from a deepening concern.

"What'll we do?"

A small waterspout kicked up in the bay only its lower vortex briefly visible before it snaked again up into the clouds.

The Dolphins chattered to each other.

"Idea, we," announced Dolphin One.

"Trust we," added Dolphin Two.

Lightning struck a palm tree and set it momentarily afire, until the rain doused it out.

The dolphins came as close as the shallows would allow.

Fontaine squatted onto her haunches and looked straight at them, her voice rising above the growl of the storm, "Please," she begged, "tell us your idea."

Chapter 9
"Seeing Things"

As she watched the agent open the door ahead of them, the thought occurred to Tiffany that with such a physique, he might well have been constructed entirely of left over steer parts in the laboratory of some mad scientist.

At least from a physical standpoint, Dan, who stood well over six feet, looked downright ordinary, as he passed the man on his way into the room that led off the hallway.

Tiffany and Ricky and Goggles followed Dan and found themselves in a rather large space that was lit just at one end, only by a fireplace.

A dozen cozy chairs surrounded a low table. And various dog pictures decorated the walls.

As the agent closed the door behind them, Ricky said, "There's no sound."

"What?" said Dan.

"Whenever I go into a room, I always notice, for professional reasons, what the ambient sounds are."

"Oh," Tiffany cooed. "You're right. No ticking clock or music or people in other rooms."

"Forget that," Ricky shot back, "the fireplace isn't even making any noise, no cozy crackling sounds."

"Maybe it's gas."

"There's plenty of ash on the hearth." He looked over at the windows. "Only rain on the glass."

"You think someone's sanitized it?" Tiffany asked him.

"It's what I'd do if I wanted to listen in on somebody or record what they were saying."

Right then, as if to make him a liar, there came from very nearby a familiar voice saying, "Damn it all, he's the only one that's got anything even remotely resembling a plan."

Tiffany thought it was probably an accidental echo or something of the like.

Then a door, well disguised as a bit of wall paneling on the other side of the room, bumped opened partway. And in the space there appeared a thin slice of movement beyond.

Directly a shiny, black nose poked through the gap.

A different male voice replied to the first, "This is a fifty-year-old problem, Mister President."

Frank and Tiffany looked quizzically at one another and strained to see what lay beyond the door.

"President Beaton?" whispered Tiffany in Dan's direction.

He nodded. And Ricky took that as a cue to shift his camera onto one of the tables and hit the start button.

Again came President Beaton's familiar voice.

"Yes, a problem which your people caused."

The black nose further opened the door; and very soon thereafter, a sleek greyhound dog entered, wearing about its neck a red and silver collar.

The President, clearly visible through the wider space, had his back turned to the folk in the adjoining room, and to Ricky's camera.

The other voice assumed a defensive tone.

"What about your people?"

A familiar-looking man stepped out from behind the President. He was saying, "If you hadn't been so greedy –"

Before she could stop herself, Tiffany blurted out, "Mister Sepaca!"

The Man saw her at once and ducked quickly out of sight.

The Secret Service escort had, since herding the four intruders into the room, hovered near the hallway door. At the sound of Tiffany's observation, the agent hurried in to block the view.

Tiffany looked at Ricky. And he winked at her.

And following on that, with a surprising promptness, the President, looking at once youthful and distinguished, came in.

The Agent closed the door tightly.

"Congressman Farrell," began the President with what seemed to be genuine good humor. "Welcome to Camp David."

Frank met the President in the center of the room and they shook hands like old friends.

"Thank you, Mister President. But it appears I'm here on a fool's errand."

The President seemed mildly surprised.

"How is that, Frank?"

"Well, sir, Mister Neil Sepaca sent me. But it turns out you two have already talked."

At that, the President seemed greatly confused. "Uh ... Frank, I do know Mister Sepaca; but he is not here."

Frank rubbed his jaw uncertainly and shifted uncomfortably under the President's steady gaze.

"Uhm, with all possible respect, sir, and unless my eyes totally deceive me, I would swear I just now caught a glimpse of the man talking with you on the other side of that doorway."

"Hmmm. Curious. Perhaps you should see an optometrist."

Then the President stepped around Frank and appraised the others people in the room.

"Ms. Diamond, of course I do recognize you; in fact I have followed your meteoric rise with great interest."

He nodded cordially to the others and said, "And I assume the guy with the camera is part of your production crew."

"Ricky Escobar, Mister President," she replied.

"Mister Escobar."

"Thank you for returning my camera, sir. Uh ... would it be okay if I shoot this?"

Without even pausing to consider the question, the President nodded.

"Fine." Then in Tiffany's direction, he added, "But nothing leaves the compound until this matter is finished."

Tiffany was obviously pleased.

"Understood, Mister President, and agreed to. You're more than generous."

"Yes I am. And my chief of staff tells me it will, of a certainty, be my eventual undoing."

He spotted Goggles.

"And you, sir, in the antique flight gear?"

"I'm their pilot," replied Goggles in a quivery voice.

"Yes. Of course you are."

And so, with the pleasantries concluded, Frank persisted in a cautious voice.

"I know what I saw."

The President gave him a hard, ungrateful look.

"The light's bad. Your eyes tricked you."

To everyone's relief, the agent picked that moment to lean in and whisper in the President's ear.

"Oh yes," the President said. And to his guests he added, "I do apologize. Be comfortable. I'll be back as soon as events allow."

With that, he, the agent and the Greyhound left the room.

Chapter 10
"No Stinkin' Answers"

Once President Beaton had left the room, the four intruders fell immediately into a chaotic babble.

"I know what I saw."

"I'm sure you're right; I saw it too; and the voice was definitely Neil Sepaca's."

"But why would he deny it?"

"And why on earth would he ever agree to let Ricky get him on video?"

"I'd like to know what he's off doing now."

And into the yammer and posturing, came Goggle's quiet voice, slightly atremble.

"Well I can tell you one thing. He scared me nearly into cardiac arrest."

He dramatically removed his unusual eye gear.

"And me with rain-spotted lenses."

He set to work polishing the glasses with his neck scarf.

Frank paced.

"Five minutes and I'm out of here."

"Patience," soothed Tiffany. "It took us hours to get here. We can afford to wait a bit longer, if it'll bring some answers."

"You expect answers from a politician?"

"You're a politician."

He was pacing again.

"Then I ought to know, right?

He stopped beside Goggles and watched as the man went on cleaning his goggle lenses.

Frank grinned mischievously.

"Always wanted to be a pilot."

He reached casually out and lifted the glasses from Goggles' hands.

"Hey, those aren't for you!"

But Frank slipped the elastic band around his head.

And immediately, he gasped, as if he had been punched hard in the stomach.

Chapter II
"The Looking Glasses"

At the very first, after Frank had settled Goggle's glasses over his face, nothing seemed much changed.

There was a rushing sound in his ears, a mixture of water and air, both under extreme pressure.

Numbers and symbols, some familiar, others unfathomably strange, scrolled at the edges of his periphery.

But in the initial second or two, what he saw out the lenses remained disappointingly normal.

After that, reality turned itself on end and ripped itself wide open.

He saw himself, a separate entity, recognizable but well out of reach.

He and President Beaton stood face to face right there in the center of the room.

The President was saying, "The light's bad. Your eyes tricked you."

It seemed to Frank that his mind was starting to turn itself wrong side out. He tried to bring his hands up to his face. But when his fingers went in search of the goggle frames, they seemed to take on the texture of limp putty.

Finally, he must have found them, because the glasses slip up on his forehead. He turned wild-eyed and looked accusingly at Goggles, who glared angrily back at him.

"I said they weren't for you. Please," he reached out a nervous hand, "you don't know the harm you're doing."

Frank's eyes remained locked with Goggles' for several seconds.

"What was it?" demanded Tiffany's voice from some great distance. "Frank?"

Without answering, Frank lowered the glasses again; and in doing so, his hand discovered that the bezels around the lenses turn.

He thought he might have heard Goggles pleading, "For mercy's sake, Mister Congressman."

But given the world into which he was sliding, he could not really be sure of anything.

Ø

The thought in Frank's head that he should, perhaps, remove the goggles came far to late for him actually to do anything about it.

By that point his mind was already miles away and more, much, much more.

In the center of the room, through the goggles, Frank saw the Secret Service Agent turn and walk backward out of the way, uncovering the President and the Greyhound standing in the open doorway. The dog retreated. The door shut.

A man's voice leaked through the door.

"Other star civilizations grew to fear the day Earth's seed would come visiting in the cosmos."

And the recognizable timber of the President's voice responded to the indictment.

"Then the crash, the alien artifacts, all of it, you're saying it was a fraud?"

A twig snapped inside the room; and something snarled at Frank.

The sound turned him quickly away from the door toward the arrangement of dog pictures on the wall. And right away the images, seen through the goggle lenses and lit only by the hearth fire, took on depth and started to move.

Coming straight at him out of the first frame, an amber-eyed wolf leaped a fallen tree dusted with snow and landed with a soft thump. A second wolf followed close behind.

From what seemed like a great distance, he heard his voice again saying, "No!"

And suddenly Frank's view changed so that it seemed that all that was happening was coming to him through the eyes of the lead wolf.

He beheld the man with the strange goggles, standing hopelessly motionless in the snow, his arm raised across his body to take the closing jaws.

At the last instant, the man jerked his head around.

Frank's gaze jumped to the next painting, a tundra landscape.

His nostrils burned and his breath made frost before his eyes. He looked down and found he had paws where his feet should have been. And a single, furtive glance over his shoulder revealed lines that harnessed him to a team of restless sled dogs.

He felt a strange sort of joy, an unfettered contentment really.

The dogs wagged their tails as a man in a parka approached with food.

He ate raw meat and found he loved the taste of blood in his mouth.

Flames replaced the snowscape; a human shape scurried past; feral dogs bared their fangs.

A Neanderthal man, cloaked in animal skins, fed wood to a fire outside a cave and offered scraps of meat to the dogs.

Then a mechanized whine grew closer carrying the sense of a distant threat with it; and it drowned out sounds of the canine feeding frenzy.

Vapory clouds filled Frank's field of vision, then quickly thinned to reveal an aerial perspective on a winter-white hillside with two wolves looking up at him.

Frank and the other wolf saw the aircraft turn toward them and soon thereafter, a bright flash lit up the dark hatchway. The other wolf yelped, jerked backward and bled in the snow.

Frank ran to the tree line, sprang over the snow, fighting the fatigue. He stopped and threw back his head.

A forlorn howl rose through the dusted pines and echoed over the sculpted ridges and came back and back again.

Ø

Reality came slowly back to Frank.

He felt something hard pressing against his back, saw flickering light out of his left periphery.

"Lie still," a garbled voice suggested, foolishly, he thought, since he had no idea how he would ever be able to move again.

Some perception of solid form swam around him. But he could not be sure it was real.

Was he on the floor? Yes, it seemed that was true. The palm of his hand, close by his side felt a coarse fiber, which he distantly reasoned must be the rug in front of the fireplace.

What a beautiful woman was she who had just bent over him.

"I think he's coming out of it," said the woman's rich alto voice. "Frank. Do you think you can sit up?"

He must have said, "Yes," because he was suddenly upright on his butt with his legs stretched straight out in front of him.

"How?" he managed to ask.

"I warned you twice about the glasses," growled Goggles.

"You fell down," said Tiffany, filling in some of the memory blanks for him. "You were shaking like you were cold; so we dragged you over here beside the fire."

They had long since removed the goggles. But it seemed Frank had not yet entirely freed himself from the visions he had beheld through the lenses.

Even as those images mixed with the shapes of the cozy room with a fireplace and good friends protectively gathered around him, he could not completely choke off a cry deep in his throat.

"Come on, Frank. Frank!"

It was Tiffany's voice reaching him through the drone of the hunters' plane.

"Look at me, Frank."

He saw her face swim above him.

"You were making weird sounds."

Goggles leaned into his periphery.

"I said it wasn't for you."

Frank glared at Goggles.

"Yes," he growled, "What the hell happened?"

Goggles shrugged.

"It's someway how the glasses let you see these little movies that the molecules store up about whatever happens to them."

He held the goggles up between them. Frank pushed them away.

"They were made for me to use," Goggles explained yet again.

Frank struggled.

"Help me get up."

Ricky and Tiffany got on either side of him.

"Okay?"

He nodded.

"On my feet."

Slowly, with all of them participating, they hoisted him to an upright stance, whereupon he seemed quickly to regain his equilibrium.

Ø

Within seconds after he had steadied himself back into a state of normalcy, Frank's eyes turned again to the goggles, now dangling from their owner's fingers.

"Let me see those again."

Goggles backed away from Frank, all the while giving him a threatening look.

"Uh-uh, no way."

"Don't worry, even I'm not dumb enough to put them on again."

He looked over at Ricky.

"Swing your camera around here." And to Goggles he added, "Let's see what happens, if you hold those things over the camera lens."

Goggles hesitated.

"Yeah, go ahead," urged Ricky.

Reluctantly, Goggles slipped the rig over the camera snout. And as they watch, the President appeared in the view finder; and bright daylight fell through the window.

Ricky walked the camera across the room. The others followed him, all eyes fixed on the view finder. Their interest mounted as the frame tightened on a strip of gold-printed circuit board in the President's hand.

Tiffany said, "Focus on the strip, Ricky."

"Turn back the bezel on the lens," prompted Frank.

As Ricky worked the goggle lens, the circuit board leaped from the President's hand and zipped away.

An instant later, in a pristine, white room, Neil Sepaca caught the board.

A door opened and a Gray entered.

Everyone around Ricky and his camera reacted with surprise.

Tiffany pointed.

"They're saying something."

Ricky cranked up the volume on the camera's built-in speakers.

The Gray was talking to Sepaca.

"Are you sure they can copy the strip?"

Sepaca replied quite matter-of-factly, "If it were any simpler, it wouldn't work."

The room around Sepaca and the Gray shuddered and the Gray intoned without noticeable concern that the magnetosphere was playing havoc with the controls.

And through the camera, they saw Sepaca slump a bit.

The Gray steadied him.

"Are you feeling all right?"

Sepaca shook his head in a definitely negative motion.

"The storm is compromising my core field. We should begin the descent while I'm able to hold the two halves together."

He carried the strip to a nearby platform, where points of bright light shone down on a crumpled disk, split on one side and scarred by extreme heat. He paused just outside the hatchway.

"Clear the landing bay."

As the Grays left, a sudden burst of energy rippled down one wall and leaped onto Sepaca. He groaned as part of him visibly peeled away into an apparently identical body. One twin fell and his mirror other half struck him a hard blow to the head.

The standing Sepaca bathed himself in the fire that fluttered over the walls and laced the chamber's interior.

Then he pried the circuit strip from his fallen twin's hand and entered the damaged disk.

As the hatchway lowered and sealed itself in place, his voice leaked out, thin and brittle.

"I have selected a human name for myself. You will call me Ator Guinard."

Ricky nearly dropped the camera.

"Madonna."

Tiffany whispered, "Dear God in heaven."

The viewfinder showed the landing bay doors opening onto a black sky.

Air rushed out.

Pulled by the escaping atmosphere, the fallen Sepaca slipped toward the opening, grabbed a strut and hung on.

Objects swirled cyclonically inside the compartment,

The disk flashed outward.

The door closed agonizingly slowly.

And within thirty seconds, calm had restored itself inside the bay.

Frank had seen enough.

For practicality's sake, he knew what he needed to know about the events that had brought him, his friends and all of humanity to their current perilous crossroads.

He drifted slowly away from the others, thinking, pondering what his next move might be – or whether any reasonable course of action against such powerful forces really did exist.

Besides, he realized with a sudden surprise, he was hearing voices. But these came not out of the camera or the adjacent room, as they had before.

He turned his head to get a better fix.

Yes, the source was definitely out there in the night of storm and bluster beyond the windows of the President's office.

The voices drew Frank to the outer wall, where the thrash of the storm grew louder.

He peered into the dark outside the cabin and at first saw only silhouettes lugging flame-filled lanterns this way and that through heavy rain.

In every case, their wanderings took them to the spot where a golf cart waited beneath a tree.

The figures bunched there.

Umbrellas gathered, welded their edges to make a temporary roof.

Someone moved enough to shift the cover and reveal two male human figures.

Something else stood there with them.

It was smaller than they.

It stood erect on long, spindly legs. It gestured with its thin arms that reach finally into the cart's back and haul out a red, metal box.

Lightning flared several times, like rapid gunfire all across the horizon.

And as the smaller figure turned and handed the box to the agent, its over-size, black eyes fixed unblinking on the cabin window, where Frank stood clearly framed.

The President looked at the window, too, and shook his head at Frank.

Then the President walked with the agent toward the cabin.

Again, lightning bands exposed the scene, glistened wetly on the tiny figure's large head and slick grey skin.

Metal glittered at its throat, some sort of a collar it seemed, all silvery and red.

The flame-filled lanterns drifted away into the rainy turmoil.

A door shut in the next room.

Frank turned from the window.

Goggles jerked the lenses off the camera.

"I believe these are mine."

Ø

An instant after Goggles had pulled the glasses from Ricky's camera lens and secreted them inside his flight jacket, the President entered with the agent, who carried the red box to the table and set it down.

The Greyhound trotted nonchalantly into view and shook water from her coat.

She looked at Frank.

By God, she seemed to wink at him.

As if to make absolutely certain he had not missed it as a fluke or passing flirtation, she did it again.

And suddenly Frank realized the President was looking back and forth from him to the box and saying, "Open it."

The Greyhound came nearer to Frank and looked up at him.

Frank looked down and smiled thinly.

"Time's not right yet, huh, girl?"

He squatted and scratched the dog's skin around her red and silvery collar.

To the President he said, "You knew my grandfather."

The President nodded.

"It's the dog made you think about him?"

Frank stroked the animal's ears.

"How he tried to stop greyhound racing."

"Yes," murmured the President. "He hated the way the breeders ran them hungry."

"Uh-huh. And starved them if they didn't perform like they wanted them to."

Tiffany's voice sounded uncommonly sharp couched in the two men's gentle musings.

"That's it?"

Except for the President, all eyes turned to look at her. He was still focused on Frank, squatting beside the dog.

"You know, Frank, lots of guys strut through that door thinking they've got all the answers."

Tiffany persisted.

"You mean all those decades ago they gave us this technology just so someday they could take it back?"

The President seems not to have heard her. He continued to address Frank.

"Most of the time, those kinds of men leave on their hands and knees.

"Mister President," nudged Tiffany.

He looked at her.

"I cannot say that. My doing so would make it true."

Lightning flashed again, several times, close beyond the window.

And this time, it was Ricky's voice that broke the silence.

"I do not think the people are so blind, sir."

Chapter 12
"Quilt Complex"

Zipper came down the stairs. He peeked around a corner from the entry hall into the kitchen.

He had expected to see the whole family there, hoped to see Sara, but found only Miriam fussing over the stove.

She smiled at him so warmly, and it came as such a surprise to him, that he thought for just a second he would almost cry.

"Good morning, Zipper."

"Morning Mrs. Burwell."

"Did you sleep soundly?"

"Yes, ma'am, I surely did. It must be the country air."

"Maybe. But I was about to guess it's a sign you have a clear conscience."

"Oh."

He was truly embarrassed. "I hardly think I could make such a presumptuous claim as all that."

"Which is probably why it might be true."

He bobbed nervously on the balls of his feet. That made her smile again

"Please sit down and we can talk a bit while I make breakfast for you."

"You don't have to do all that."

"It is my joy to serve you."

"Thank you. I really enjoy hearing you talk, the sound of your voice. I never knew my mother."

He took a chair.

"She died?'

"I guess. I got adopted; but I got separated from my parent."

"I'm sorry."

"It's okay."

He looked around.

"Where is everybody?"

Her sweet face warmed the room again.

"Oh there's big happenings down at the barn. Sara's mare is about to foal."

"Foal?"

She nodded as she scrambled four eggs.

"Arabella, the mare, is having a baby this morning. You should stop by the barn on your way to the meadow."

He made a small, doubtful face.

She laughed like tiny bells tinkling.

"It's the sort of thing that, once you've seen it happen, it can change your life forever."

"Yes ma'am."

"Here you go."

She set the eggs and toast and bacon and sliced tomatoes in front of him. And he began to eat, rather ravenously it seemed.

She had gone to a far corner of the room and was returning with several squares of cloth held lightly between her fingers.

"Did you know Amish women like to make quilts for people they like, Zipper?"

He paused as if the very asking of the question has surprised him.

"Uhm … yes ma'am, I do seem to recall knowing that from some place."

"Well … without sounding too prideful, I'd ask you what you think of these."

She laid the cloth squares out on the table near his plate for his consideration.

"Oh my gosh," he gurgled.

The squares, about a dozen of them, were representational of the tattoos on Zipper's forearms.

"They're wonderful. You made these?"

"Yes. Do you like them?"

"They look just like my skin art."

"If you agree, I'll make enough of them to fashion a quilt for you."

He laid down his fork and stared at his plate.

"Nobody ever did anything like that for me before."

She laid her hand over his and said, "I'm sure your mother loved you, Zipper. I'm guessing she had no choice but to find you a safe place to grow up."

"I guess."

"Would you like me to finish the quilt?"

"I would, yes ma'am."

Ø

By the time Zipper came out the front door and into the farmyard, the sun had cleared the treetops around the grand house; and he was feeling really good, about everything.

So, en route to where the machine sat, over the tunnel down in the meadow, he made a small, arching detour that carried him past the barn.

As he approached, he heard Seth's voice, pitched with an uncommon species of anger, coming from inside.

"My family and I have shared our good fortune with you and all the others we've offered shelter during this perilous time. Some, like you, have taken unfair advantage. You did not have to steal the milk or abuse the cow or skitter the horse in that stall who is at this moment on the verge of giving birth."

"We thought it was all here for any one of us to use if we needed it," came another voice, thin and whiny. "We never knew you Quaker type people was so possessive."

Zipper peeked inside and saw Seth, with Sara standing only a little behind him, faced off with two young men, an oddball couple, one tall and skinny, the other short and meaty.

Seth pointed a forefinger at the pair of them.

"Leave this farm now; brush the dust of your having stayed here off the soles of your shoes; and never return."

The meaty one drew himself up as much as gravity would allow and inquired in a vaguely threatening voice, "And what if we choose not to vacate the premises, so to speak?"

At that point, Zipper thrust himself through the door and, in as intimidating a voice as he could muster said, "Morning, Mister Burwell. Some kind of a problem I could help you with?"

"Doing just fine, Zipper."

"Just so everybody knows I'm here."

The two men conducted a short estimate of Zipper and apparently decided he looked entirely too freaky to be easily intimidated.

"Fine," whined the long, skinny type. "Good riddance anyway. We'll do just hunky-dory without you holier than thou sob sisters."

They left the barn then, giving Zipper a generous berth on their way out.

When they were well gone, Seth squinted at Zipper.

"Would you really have done them harm?"

"Despite how I may look to you sometimes, or make you feel, Mister Burwell, I've only been in one fight in my entire life."

Zipper looked over at Sara and seemed more than a little reluctant to finish the story he had started.

"I knocked the other guy down and he hit his head. Wasn't seriously hurt. But when I thought what might have happened, it scared me really bad."

From nearby, there came the sound of a living thing in distress.

"It's Arabella," gasped Sara.

They all hurried to a nearby stall, where a beautiful roan horse lay on her side, whinnying and snorting softly. She raised her head as the humans arrived on the scene.

And over the next twenty minutes, as Zipper looked on, Sara stroked Arabella's head and sang to her some songs in what must have been German.

Sara looked up at Zipper.

"Arabella means 'Beautiful Eagle'. She is beautiful, isn't she?"

Zipper nodded in awe and watched, as in almost reverent silence, Seth aided the splendid creature in completing a process her species had accomplished on its own, in the wild, for tens of thousands of years before ever a human set astride an equine back.

Arabella licked the foal clean.

He was a colt, as perfect as his mother.

When first he stood on wobbly legs, he immediately passed wind.

The three of them laughed.

Sarah named him Thunder.

Chapter 13
"Hydrogen-1, Helium-2+"

When Zipper came down the path that led from the break in the fence and into the meadow, he found Fish standing beside the tunnel mouth that lead under the Machine.

And Fish was clearly quite angry.

"Where the hell have you been?" he demanded.

"Something wrong?"

Fish motioned Zipper into the tunnel.

Zipper scurried quickly through the passage beneath the meadow grass, and popped his head up from the hole under the Machine.

As he brushed a little dirt out of his long hair, he quickly noticed that the virus encryption was no longer showing on the display, having been replaced, it seemed, by some sort of a travelogue.

As Fish came in beside him, a voice from the machine narrated the action on the screen.

"On the Ile De La Cite, we find the spot where Paris began during the second Iron Age, more than two thousand years ago."

Zipper stared blankly for a second or two, then checked all the connections and finally leaned back, clearly disheartened.

"I don't get it," he whispered. "It was working last night."

"Here, in the very heart of the City of Lights," continued the narrator, "one comes upon the famous Zero Mile, a bronze plaque from which the distances for all the roads in France are reckoned."

Zipper picked up the cube-shaped keypad from the red box and worked the same pattern as before.

Nothing changed.

"Modern-day visitors find pleasant tree-lined quays along with such historic structures as the Palais de Justice and Notre-Dame Cathedral."

"Can't you shut it off?" begged Fish.

Zipper fingered the controls.

"And if the visitor tires of those visual riches, he need stroll only a short distance east to the river bank for a stunning view of the Arc de Triomphe and the Eiffel Tow—"

Suddenly the presentation stopped.

The Machine's own voice cut in.

"An error has occurred. Connector path hydrogen-1, helium-2+ no longer exists. Check 1-2+ shunt and reapply."

Fish practically scream, "What in hell is a 1-2+ shunt?!"

Zipper pointed to markings along the Machine's underside.

"I was awake in physics class long enough to know hydrogen has one electron like that sign; and helium has two, like that one."

Fish spit on his thumb and cleaned the metal.

"There. Those two holes. Something must have gone between them."

They dropped immediately and thoroughly searched the dirt on the tunnel's floor.

"How on earth could we possibly know what a shunt is supposed to look like?!" demanded Zipper.

Fish fairly roared, "How the hell should I know?!"

Zipper eased back on his haunches.

"Only thing."

Fish's eyes narrowed into slits.

"What?"

"Stay cool man."

"What were you going to say?"

Zipper thought a second or two longer and shrugged.

"If you or me didn't take it, then somebody else made an awful lucky guess."

"Uh-huh, my thinking exactly," agreed Fish, as he stood there staring at Zipper.

"What?" said Zipper.

"Since I didn't steal it, you little freakoid –"

"I hate it when you call me that."

"Freakoid!

They lunged at each other in the tunnel; and as the struggle grew more violent, they dislodged a number of the roof supports, which let dirt fall in and seal their way out.

"Oh god," moaned Fish as he began clawing at the fill. "I can't stand confined spaces."

Chapter 14
"Second Choice"

In the absence of light pollution, the Milky Way galaxy, the greater part of it as seen from Earth's vantage point way out in Orion's arm, made a lacy tracing of stars across the sky.

The moon was busy elsewhere at the moment.

There was no light; there were no shadows.

Sounds replaced vision.

Something metallic went "snip" in the darkened world. Another "snipping" sound followed, and a dozen more after that.

No one spoke.

No stones turned or rattled under a careless boot sole.

Snip.

Shank felt Magwood's hand on his elbow, guiding him past a cut through a chain-link and barbed-wire fence.

Neither Shank nor Odenwelder had night vision specs, so they were blind and totally encased in the inky night.

They relied on Magwood and his men to guide them.

That had, of course, been the case from the very beginning of their union, all the way from Montana forests into Arizona badlands.

Now they stood in the infrared shade of a massive concrete block.

Shank thought how lonely it was, even with two dozen other humans within easy arm's reach. They were so quiet, not even the betrayal of a breath taken in or exhaled.

He, Shank, might easily have been there all by himself.

Then Magwood whispered, "The door's over there."

Two men produced packets and stuck them to a spot where the door must surely have been.

There it was a brief sound, like a sofa cushion dropped onto the floor from a low height.

Poof.

"Door's blown," Magwood announced, this time in something less than a whisper.

He caught Shank's elbow again and they moved.

Shank knew somebody else was leading Odenwelder.

"Stairwell."

That would have been Magwood again.

"Foot down."

Shank felt the edge with his toe.

Down they went through pitch blackness.

Shank counted twenty-five steps.

And someone below finally lit a lamp. Others did the same; and they attached the lights magnetically to their helmets.

"Control room's at the bottom, turn right."

Shank turned and saw Magwood grinning at him and Odenwelder.

"We're in, boys. Your show, now."

Multiple light beans swept the walls all the way to the bottom.

There came a minor bump of a sound, more felt through their soles than heard.

The control room door was gone in a swirl of smoke.

Magwood, Shank and Odenwelder reached the bottom ahead of the others and, so, were the first inside the room, which, as it turned out, was surprisingly small, given the number of equipment racks crammed into it.

Some of the cases stood partly empty.

Magwood took a few seconds to orient himself. Then he pointed into a shadowy corner.

"Radar ought to be over that way."

They circled to a pair of dark cabinets and checked out the power couplers.

Shank looked at it carefully and let out a half of a laugh.

"Oh man, this stuff is sure-enough, genuine antique."

Odenwelder leaned in.

"Must be sorta like being on an archeological dig."

Magwood looked worried in the strong cross light of the lanterns.

"You guys can make it work, though, right?"

Odenwelder held the red box up between him and Shank.

"What do you think?" Shank asked him.

"What I think is that we lose nothing to open the box now."

They hesitate.

Shank suggested, "We should clean our hands first to make sure the fingerprints take."

They did.

Then after another brief pause full of dread, Shank worked the eye scan. Odenwelder did the same thing; and the box opened.

Carefully picking through the innards, Odenwelder lifted out the chocolate bar, which connected to a fat cable that had a silvery glove-like object dangling from its opposite end.

Shank's spirits sank; and his voice reflected that feeling.

"No stinkin' cigar."

The longer Odenwelder examined the cable and the glove, the angrier he became.

"What's this supposed to be -- some kind of a joke? Damn glove's too small for my hand."

Shank checked out the dangling fingers and the width of the palm and wrist opening.

"Me, too."

"So, who could Sepaca have meant it for? This is ridiculous, letting us come this far, risking our lives, him all the time knowing we wouldn't be able to use the device inside the box."

As Odenwelder had been grousing, Magwood had busied himself, examining the glove. He slipped his fingers tentatively inside the wrist opening, then inserted his entire hand.

Immediately, the glove began to glow warmly.

"Damn. Would you look at that!"

Shank was mildly horrified.

"This is not a game. Take it off."

Magwood gave him a hurt look, then tugged at the wrist band. Nothing moved. He grasped each of the fingers and the thumb and tried to roll the thing off his hand, all to no avail.

"It's stuck!"

"Jeez," Shank wailed pitifully.

He and Odenwelder tried to help Magwood. And in their struggle to remove the glove, they chanced to maneuver Magwood's hand near what must have been the power connector for the entire control room, because the equipment bays and the ceiling lights all flickered on then off again.

"Wait," said Odenwelder. "Put your hand back there where it was."

Magwood complied; and Odenwelder shoved the plug into the palm of his gloved hand. Instantly, the entire room lit up again.

And they all cheered.

Odenwelder, always a practical man, yelled out, "Somebody start timing – we've got twenty-four hours."

Chapter 15
"Space Port"

The sun looked quite like an angry hole seared through an otherwise faultless sky, for all purposes, a nasty cigarette burn.

A wall of sand, at least a mile high, rose in the distance, headed, by good fortune, in a direction likely to carry it safely away from the five horses and their riders, as they moved at a trot across the low, flat plain.

Equine hooves cut deep into the fragile varicose topsoil. They raised a fine dust that hung low in the air, thinning almost at once to transparency and settling invisibly.

Kimama and Akando had taken the lead early on, nine sweaty, gritty hours ago, as the four of them left the reservation and rode hard to this point, where there were faded signs that identified the land as property of the U.S. government and forbade all unauthorized passage over it.

Under the circumstances, such a proscription seemed patently silly; and Strong said so.

"As if those signs would discourage anyone with hostile intent against the U.S. Government."

In fact she and Dan Diamond riding with the pack horses near the rear of the small caravan, had just begun their descent of a shallow rise, when a squad of armed and uniformed soldiers ran out to block their way.

"Halt where you are and step down!" yelled one of the men who wore a major's gold clusters on his collar.

"Everybody dismount," ordered Strong.

The four of them stepped down immediately from their mounts.

The soldiers quickly encircled them.

Alison Strong stepped out to the front of her party.

"Major," she addressed the officer. "I am Colonel Alison Strong."

The man was already wide-eyed.

"Yes, ma'am, I recognize you."

He seemed to realize he had forgotten to salute and did so at once.

"These people are with me." Strong told him. "Where would I find General Atkins?"

"Got stuck off someplace in all this mess, ma'am. I'm the Exec, Major Petty. If you'll come this way, I can at least get you and your party out of this damned heat."

"We'd really appreciate that, Major Petty."

They all set off walking toward a high, rocky bulwark located about a quarter mile away.

Along the way, Strong said to Perry, "What I'm hoping, Major, is that you're gonna tell me there's a VentureStar sitting on a launch pad waiting to go."

They left the horses with the soldiers and climbed broad concrete steps to the bulwark's top.

"Got one on the pad," he told her. "But I'm afraid, ma'am, that her tanks're only about three-quarters full."

"Any way to top 'em off?"

"Yes ma'am, emergency hand pumps. But that's gonna take the better part of three hours."

Just then, they stepped out onto the flat top of the bulwark, which entirely circled a mile-wide crater that snuggly contained five launch pads.

And on one of them there sat a graceful white and black space machine.

Strong nodded, as much at the beauty of the craft as to acknowledge the exec's guesstimate.

"Then you'd better get your men busy, Major."

"Yes ma'am."

He snapped a salute, spun about, and ran off shouting orders to everyone within hearing distance.

He descends a series of steps built down the inside of the crater wall and disappeared into the shadows at its depths.

In watching him go, Strong almost missed Dan's voice at her elbow.

"Alison."

"Yes."

She turned and saw Dan, Kimama and Akando staring wide-eyed at a point somewhere behind her.

And when Strong glanced back over her right shoulder, she found herself looking at Neil Sepaca, who stood only feet away, wavering slightly, mystically in the hot air.

Akando reassured himself.

"There's no such thing as ghosts."

Strong took her time.

"But more than our fair share of illusions, I'd say."

She moved her arm through the Sepaca image, as if to satisfy herself that even though it was there, he was not solidly real.

"The locater signals integrated into each of your power packs confirm that you have all activated them and that each of your teams has now arrived at its assigned operational point."

Chapter 16
"He's Everywhere!"

The unexpected appearance of Sepaca's image inside the observatory dome interrupted Louise Padget and Hollis Cryer just at they were about to begin the process of removing the eyepiece from the great reflecting telescope.

Sepaca, convincing except for a slight fuzziness around his edges, seemed to be standing only a few feet away near the huge motorized mount.

"As quickly as possible," he continued, "and with appropriate care, you should complete your final preparations."

Ø

The scene at the Sandy Cove Retirement Complex in Florida had assumed much the same feel, although Sepaca had a larger audience there.

All the Square Dancers along with Natalie Misaka and Paul Grigsby surrounded Sepaca's image. And nobody seemed to notice the whish, whish, whish the phonograph needle made on a record that had played through to the label.

Sepaca was telling them, "The mathematics team should begin their calculations now using this moment as their Epoch Time."

From somewhere outside the range of the scanners that captured his image for transit, he plucked a futuristic-looking clock and held it up for them to see.

The Square Dancers all carefully synchronized their watches.

Ø

Down beneath the earth, inside the Nike base control room, Sepaca's image was a little worsened for its passage through several layers of concrete and steel.

When he first appeared, Magwood temporarily dropped the power connector from his metal-gloved hand and the lights winked out.

But Sepaca remained there in the room glowing faintly, life size, though occasionally throughout the transmission, an arm or a leg, and once, even his head, disappeared altogether.

But his voice consistently came through quite clearly.

"Likely intermittent communications lapses will require a certain amount of personal initiative on the part of teams and their individual members."

Shank called out, "Magwood!" and the commandant scooped up the connector so that the lighted control panels came back to life again.

Ø

The great storm slapped vengefully at the cove, as if its very existence and humanity's tenuous mark on it had made of it an effrontery that was somehow responsible for the loss of what peace and normalcy had existed there before.

Wind drove a vicious rain against a pre-fab metal building, eventually folding and breaking it and sending its parts tumbling down to the shore, where waves battered them against jagged rocks.

Lightning blazed, sizzled the water to a soup that almost hid a bit of flickering light from a subsurface cave opening, a glow that wove its way into the sandy currents and became a part of them.

Within the cavern, Alvin Farrell and Ursula Fontaine, both wearing SCUBA gear, bobbed with the Dolphins near a spot where

Sepaca's image stood messiah-like on the water's surface, his head all but touching the rough, low ceiling.

"Expect surprises to arise, "he told them all, wherever they were. "Use your special talents to turn the problems into opportunities."

Ø

There fell a light drizzle on the Burwell farm up in northern Pennsylvania, not much as rain might be gauged in that part of the country, but enough to condense on the Machine's shell, whatever that composition might be, and run under the flat belly, so that it dripped and dripped on Fish and Zipper, already miserable, in the hole beneath the infernal alien field generator.

Fish angrily whipped off his glasses and, after tugging his shirt tail out from inside his trousers, used it to wipe the wet off the lenses.

Zipper sat only a little more composed and less miserable on the other side of the hole

Between them there flickered Sepaca's image.

"Earth is a spectacular world, humanity a wonder of generosity and creative beauty that may exist nowhere else in the entire universe."

Zipper toyed absently with a ringed ear piercing, and managed to scowl at Fish, as the cantankerous fellow replaced the spectacles aride his nose.

"We must keep genuine faith with one another," Sepaca told his squads everywhere. "And we must do all that events require, not just for ourselves, but for generations not yet even dreamed of."

After that, the image remained briefly in place, then it fluttered and quickly vanished.

Zipper nodded, apparently having agreed just short of shouting out, "Amen."

He did say, "He said it right, Fish, about creative beauty."

Fish was still fidgeting, loosening his collar, apparently to relieve some minor trouble he was having with his breathing.

"You're some kind of expert on that, are you?"

Zipper looked a little hurt.

"I just saw a baby horse get born. Mrs. Burwell says a thing like that changes a person forever. And I think she's right."

Chapter 17
"Hide And Seek"

Except for a fairly loud mosquito hum inside Guinard's flying disk, there was no sense of velocity or vibration at all, nothing that might suggest the craft was at that very moment involved any sort of active function.

It was, in fact, traveling at multiples of the speed of sound that were in terms of human technology astoundingly exponential.

On the flight deck, Guinard turned from the holographic globe, where a yellow light flashed out of existence somewhere in the mid-Atlantic Ocean.

The Priest smiled as he peeked timidly over Guinard's shoulder.

"You've found Sepaca?"

Guinard's annoyed exhalation sounded like vented steam.

"Fool. He is now ready to be found."

Outside, with the air along the hull frictioned into fee ozone, the disk banked, severely altered its course and sped on its way to a showdown rendezvous.

Chapter 18
"Strong Is the Best"

The spaceport inside the artificial crater at the Harper Dry Lake Complex was acrawl with the uncommon business that only precedes an imminent launch.

Several crews scurried up and down the gantry and in shouting voices relayed final-check data from one swarm to the next.

Dan Diamond, Akando and Kimama, all outfitted in silver flight suits, stood at the service tower's base, leaned back, and looked up the full length of the VentureStar.

Kimama said, "It never looks this big on TV."

At her elbow, Akando whistled.

"That is so right. And the woman, Strong, she will fly this amazing machine?"

Dan slapped him reassuringly on the back.

"She's pretty amazing herself, Akando, an ace pilot."

"Good?"

"Just about the best."

Kimama made a small face.

"I still haven't heard exactly what it is we're supposed to be involved in while she's doing all this flying."

Dan laughed.

"For that part of it, you'll mostly be doing the same thing as me. That would mean staying out of Colonel Strong's way as much as possible."

He looked over his shoulder and spotted Strong walking toward them in something of a hurry.

"Without a full crew," he finished, "Colonel Strong's gonna need some extra hands to help out."

Strong and Major Petty climbed the steps to the launch pad's first level and paused beside Dan and Kimama and Akando.

Strong carried the red box.

Perry was saying, "I still don't see how you're going to power this baby up."

"Being as how I'm not real sure myself, that makes two of us. But being a betting lady, I'll lay odds that's already been worked out; and it's gonna happen as planned."

She turned her cool eyes then on Dan, Kimama and Akando.

"Let's get climbing, children. Seems like we've got us some serious alien butt-kickin' to do."

With that, she started up the ladder; and the others quickly follow.

Ø

Once they had gained the VentureStar's flight deck, Strong crawled beneath the engineering control panel and, lying flat on her back, uncoupled the main power bus.

She gave it a critical appraisal.

"Time to pony up, Cowboys. Come here, Dan'l and lend us your fingerprint."

She and Dan quickly went through the process of pressing the prescribed platelet on the box and looking into the laser.

And as soon as the box sprung its top, she dragged out the chocolate bar and gave it a long, hard inspection.

Dan, Kimama and Akando, cradling Iye, leaned in close for a look on their own.

Strong glanced up at them all.

"Everybody happy?"

"Perfect," pronounced Dan, and added, "to no one's surprise."

Kimama and Akando nodded.

"Let's do it, then," Strong said, as she snapped the two halves together.

Immediately the ship powered up.

Strong climbed up off the floor and plopped down into the pilot's couch.

"Okay, Dan'l, you and me check her out."

And to Kimama and Akando she said, "And while we're doing that, you guys can get busy stowing all this stuff in the lockers."

With that, Kimama and Akando gathered up all the packs and other items they had brought along and toted them to the cabin's rear.

To Strong, Dan said confidentially said, "Without a com link to the other teams, we're going out on a limb here, in more ways than one."

She nodded her head.

"Yep. But we've gotta go and hope for the best."

He snapped her a sharp salute.

"Aye, aye, Captain."

... part four

"The jaws of darkness
do devour it up;
So quick bright things
come to a confusion."
William Shakespeare

Chapter I
"Citadel of Light"

As the ground crews ran from the gantry, the tower folded away from beside the VentureStar and left it sitting there unfettered, sculpted steel and super compositions, glistening whitely in the bright sun.

There evolved transient disturbances in the sands beyond the buttress wall that surrounded the cratered complex.

Wind sounds, so it seemed.

Major Petty looked worried.

Some of it could, perhaps, be just natural wind sheers or thermal bursts. But there was definitely something else, too, a faint, guttural chatter, that hovered just barely within the range of human hearing.

"On your toes!" he shouted to his men. "This may be the most important thing any of us has ever done or ever will do!"

The sounds, more than one, came from the near distance; and they echoed a familiar cadence.

The guys at ground level looked at their Major. They had heard it before in jungles and deserts. They definitely knew what it was.

In full battle rattle, they scurried to the walls just in time to see four black dots slide through a saddle between two buttes. The dots were coming straight on.

Four black ACRONYM helicopters.

Well-trained crews in fortified ground emplacements opened up withering anti-aircraft fire directed at the choppers.

Strong looked out the VentureStar's windows and saw the battle starting up.

"Buckle up!"

Her hands leaped across the controls.

And a second later, a hundred feet down, the area immediately beneath the aero-spike engine blossomed fire; and the space ship raised itself slowly off its pad.

The helicopters came straight on, closing the gap. One released a missile that made a straight line for the VentureStar.

Some quick-witted soul on the ground fired a series of flares that arced to one side, spewing chaff as it went and distracting the missile off its course.

An anti-aircraft battery nearby earned its pay with a strike that brought a trail of smoke from one of the choppers.

The VentureStar, still moving agonizingly slow, gathered momentum.

More flares rose between the helicopters and the launch pad and confused another pair of missiles.

Material on the gantry tower caught fire.

An incoming missile locked on that heat signature and blew away its middle, leaving the rest to fall in a spectacular, flaming heap.

The VentureStar, by then a tiny white toy tauntingly high in the sky, rolled lazily onto its back and streaked away on a tail of smoke and fire.

The wounded chopper, trailing oily smoke, crashed, skidded and burned. The others turned away.

Chapter 2
"The Group Of Seven"

Since the residents of the Sandy Cove Retirement Complex had assembled themselves in the out of doors, there were, in abundance, the ambient sounds of nature.

The surf advanced and retreated gently, unobtrusively, over sand and stone.

The palm fronds made arrhythmic castanet clickings high over where the tables, usually reserved for bingo and craft sessions, had been arranged in neat columns.

Birds sang; insects buzzed; occasionally somebody coughed.

Otherwise, out there on the grassy commons, all lay expectantly, tensely silent.

There were seven groups of them on that one corner of the green, drawn up as near as possible to the cove's edge.

One member of each team wore a MINDMELD scalp mesh on his head, the power lines for each running into a router that was, itself, mated to an extension of the chocolate bar.

Natalie Misaka and Paul Grigsby moved from group to group, where slide rules flashed in wrinkled, often arthritic fingers, and ball point pens scratch furiously on paper pads.

Teams at tables labeled Epoch, Orbital Inclination, Right Ascension of Ascending Node, Argument of Perigee, Eccentricity, Mean Motion, and Mean Anomaly, all fed their figures to the MINDMELD wearers.

The water inside the cove glowed a rich amber across its surface. And down in its depth, fireflies seem to dance and dart in every direction.

Chapter 3
"Light Show"

Dusty sunlight fell in through the observatory door, slashed across the concrete floor, and bumped its way over the red box that sat open between Louise Padget and Hollis Cryer.

Into an opening on the telescope barrel that was usually occupied by the astronomer's eyepiece, she had just begun to thread a cylindrical device that was a perfect fit in size and groove pattern.

Then Cryer plugged an umbilical trailing off the just-installed instrument into the chocolate bar; and brilliant light filled the telescope's long, fat length.

There inside the dome, it made for a spectacular display.

But that was nothing when compared to the show that leaped out the open section of the observatory dome.

A brilliantly white and dancing braid of light shot out from the telescope's open end and cut its way through the empty blue sky.

Chapter 4
"Keeping Track"

Deep under a field of boulders in a tortured landscape just short of the Colorado Rockies, the abandoned Nike missile base was, ironically, one of the few places in the world that enjoyed more than enough light.

Shank and Odenwelder were busy, their heads shoved into either side of an equipment rack, adjusting, fine tuning the station's radar equipment.

So far, the screens with their sweeping bands of color showed nothing of interest at all.

Shank nervously ruffled his hair.

"Where's that damned com link?"

Ø

Ever since Sepaca's image had vanished from inside the underwater cave, Farrell and Fontaine had had little do other than bob about in the rough water with the two talkative Dolphins.

"When start we, humans?" asked Dolphin Two in her sweet squeaky voice.

"Hopefully soon," Fontaine answered, with just the slightest hint of worry in her voice.

Dolphin One's sensitive receptors seemed to detect her tonal difference.

"Or never start at all?" he asked.

"Soon," Farrell assured him in a brighter voice. "We will start soon."

Chapter 5
"I See You!"

There raced across the ocean waters a shadow that constantly changed its outline with the varied shapes of the waves and troughs.

The sleek and shiny disk which the umbra swam beneath and kept a constant pace with, was the very same beast that carried, undigested in its belly, Guinard, his ecclesiastical lieutenant, righteously swathed in ebony robes, and an sizable force of heavily-armed troopers.

On the mezzanine above the strapped-in mercenaries, the Priest studied a holographic globe upon which a disk icon, not unlike their own craft, closed rapidly behind a flashing yellow dirigible.

Close by, Guinard touched a control that soundlessly rolled metal covers from over a convex windscreen just above where they stood.

The Priest recoiled briefly as undiluted sunlight flooded in and at the dizzying speed of their advance.

Guinard seemed completely unaffected. He pressed yet another button that slowed the disk's speed.

The Priest squinted, then pointed through the open air beyond the thick transparency.

"There," he gurgled, as if Guinard could not see it well enough for himself.

"Yes-s-s-s." hissed Guinard.

Sky Haven lay just ahead.

Chapter 6
"Cloudy Forecast"

Where only clear sky had existed before, there had just appeared, all within a mere thirty seconds, a string of nascent cloud patches, thirteen of them, with wide empty spaces separating each from the next.

Strangely, they all shuffled about constantly, like some sort of an aerial shell game.

No doubt all of them had been artificially created.

Moreover, there existed, as an equal certainty, the fact that all but one drifted about as empty decoys.

The game provided absolutely no room for error, of course.

It was up to the hunter to pick the right formation from amongst the baker's dozen; and he had to get it right the first time out.

As quarries had always done since the dawn of terrestrial life, Sepaca would wait, hold his breath and hope to catch his opponent looking in some other direction.

If he could do that, then he and Guinard would suddenly have changed places; and that army sealed inside the disk would become the quarry; and they would have to run and hide.

Which puff and swirl held Sky Haven?

One could not tell by looking.

There was, of course, technology to see inside those clouds. And as evolution had always decreed, there also existed the wherewithal to blind the seer's sharpest electronic eyes.

How to choose?

Chapter 7
"Gates Of Hell"

Waiting was something Sepaca had always been good at.

His Captain Stackhouse was more aggressive. He had already brought the dirigible down low against the water. And he had turned the great ship broadside to the disk's last recorded path of approach.

He was anxious to see the battle joined.

As planned, a buoy set loose inside a nearby drift emitted a creaky sound, some metal-on-metal signature designed to betray quite falsely, yet with canny accuracy, a mechanical presence swathed in floating concentrations of sun-warmed sea water.

The buoy creaked again, a bit differently the second time around.

And then the sky lit brightly.

Guinard had attacked the buoy.

Another flash washed through the thick haze, closer than the first, yet still harmlessly distant.

Stackhouse nodded at Sepaca and pointed straight off their starboard side.

"You're sure?" whispered Sepaca.

Stackhouse nodded certainly.

Without actually speaking, Sepaca mouthed the word, "Fire!"

And the gates of hell suddenly flung themselves wide open.

Chapter 8
"Smoke And Loud Noises"

Yellow fire still foamed around and inside the cloud bank in which Captain Stackhouse had planted an aerial buoy with the decoy dirigible sounds.

The disk had drawn to a full-stop hover in order to launch a second device to finish the job.

But already, from another formation somewhat distant from the first, a lethal barrage of high-voltage energy had just begun to rake and slam the disk.

Inside that cloud, every gun blister all along Sky Haven's port flank had opened fire and had set up a near wall of intense heat and light around the unseen disk.

Their accuracy was amazing.

The disk shook and shed bits of its sheathing. Immediately it lost its stationary advantage, moving drunkenly first one way, then the other, dropping, bobbing up again.

Things inside were just as chaotic, wobbling and shuddering.

A trooper lost his helmet which clattered around the lower part of the crew section, finally smacking one man in the face, knocking him limp inside his harness and setting his nose and mouth to bleeding.

Without apparent command, an arm swung down from overhead and sprayed a foam across the man's wounds that stopped the blood flow and restored the skin at once.

Bang! Boom! Bang!

A giant hand seemed to shake the disk as if it had no real mass, no station at all in the universe.

Another man vomited; and his digestive spoils churned and splattered in every direction, some even slinging itself up to the flight deck, where Guinard struggled to maintain his footing.

The Priest, in his hurry to wipe away the sick that had landed on him, fell with a profound thump that left him breathless and unable to stop a full-speed slide that carried him hard against a bulkhead.

The man wept and assumed a crawling posture as he went in search of some sort of a hand hold.

Guinard laughed in a state of pure fury.

"Off your knees, Monsignor, it's too late now for your dusty prayers."

He worked the controls with one fist while holding himself in place with the other.

Chapter 9
"Mortal Wounds"

In Guinard's able hands, his craft turned itself askew to the ocean below, making the craft a more difficult target for the gunnery squads inside that cloud bank.

The disc's own artillery pumped bursts wildly into the formation, which had grown so heated and energized by the fighting that it was quickly changing into a storm cell.

When lightning flashed inside, an elongated shadow appeared on the hazy cloud wall.

The disk continued to fire as it swept around the dirigible's projection. The blasts seem aimed mostly at the craft's rear section.

In seconds, rounds struck each of Sky Haven's three giant props, sending blades and bits of drive shaft flying in every direction.

The disk whipped on around to the dirigible's starboard side and immediately fell under the heaviest fire yet.

The disk skated sideways and dipped and bobbed, actually hit the water and sank immediately out of sight.

Ø

Following its own bubbles toward the depths, the disk twisted and passed beneath the dirigible's gliding shadow, thrown on the ocean surface by the lightning flashes at work within the cloud.

Inside the disc, as loose objects flew freely in every direction, the troopers remained harnessed in their individual niches.

Above them, bubbles swirled around the wind screen transparency.

Guinard clung to the control panels and flew the disk.

The Priest, with a deep but bloodless cut on his forehead, cringed in terror.

"Oh god of the deep, deliver thou thy humble servants."

Guinard laughed a banshee cackle.

"Pray, pray, pray!" he shouted.

Daylight flashed yet again through the water-streaked wind screen.

The ocean surface broke.

The disk shot straight up out of the water right into a hail of weapons fire from the drifting dirigible.

The force of the barrage flipped the disk like a loose coin.

Light and darkness, water and sky took their turns spinning past the rolling wind screen.

Guinard danced his fingers over a string of red buttons.

Inside the cloud they went. Energy beams, too many to count, darted from the speedy disk at the slow-moving dirigible.

Fires broke out along Sky Haven's great length, followed by a series of secondary explosions.

And slowly, one by one, the gun bubbles went dark and the weapons fire fell totally silent.

The disk continued to circle, blasting away at every battery, until the dirigible hung dark and unresponsive in the charged air.

Chapter 10
"Trooper Scooper"

Inside the disc, the harnesses snapped loose from around the troopers.

They broke as a single wave from their niches and with a feral scream, rushed toward an opening hatchway.

And as the two craft danced in a floating embrace along an indeterminate course above the waves, a part of the disc folded out to form a ramp.

Guinard's troopers stormed across it and smashed their way into Sky Haven's gondola.

One trooper, apparently hit by fire from inside the dirigible, tumbled from the ramp, vanishing from sight before he ever hit the water.

Behind the troopers, Guinard dragged the Priest out from under a console and hauled him toward the hatch. The Priest touched the dry cut on his head.

"I'm hurt."

When Guinard and the Priest came out onto the ramp, the Priest saw the churning water below, and he teetered, it seemed, on the verge of losing consciousness.

But Guinard would not let him be. He snatched the man up by his collar and dragged him roughly the rest of the way to the gondola.

Chapter II
"All In The Eyes"

Guinard and the Priest came into the cavernous reception bay through a smashed window.

The space was by then totally deserted, as the battle drifted from the gondola into other parts of the ship, its sounds reaching them from a distance.

Guinard shook the Priest.

"Bring my Oracle here at once."

The Priest was too exhausted to resist.

One of his eyes rolled immediately back into it socket, revealing a hole cut through the white, from where the tip of something shiny squirmed into view.

"My hailing signals have all been ignored," the Priest told Guinard.

A metallic tendril snaked from the eyeball, flicking a forked probe from its tip. The Priest's other eye telescoped from its socket and oscillated a frosty light in the air near the tendril.

Guinard kicked a fallen, moaning trooper.

"Then force contact, Holy Man. Do it now."

The tendril arched and drove itself into the light; and as it did so, it progressively disappeared.

Chapter 12
"Slither Thither"

Midnight at midday, a typhoon-induced phenomenon that lay crushingly heavy across the idyllic inlet.

A hard rain pounded the shoreline, where an orange flotation device bobbed to the surface in a trough between two waves.

A black cable trailed out the floater's side and down into the churn of water and buoyant debris.

The cable twisted one way and the other as it followed gravity downward from the surface, lay snake-like over some bottom-side formations and finally disappeared through the dark mouth of an underwater cave.

There had not been much to keep Farrell and Fontaine busy since Sepaca's image flickered and vanished from there inside the tiny hollow.

They had long since placed suction-cup sensors on the dolphins' foreheads and run the links to an electronic box, powered by one of the chocolate bars, all of which sat on a rocky ledge away from the wet.

Sudden chatter from the Dolphins turned Farrell and Fontaine around, just as a metal tentacle twisted out at them through an anomalous patch of Arctic-blue that lay flat as a coat of paint against the overhang.

Dolphin One squeaked, "Bad light!"

His tail flukes carried him backward from the intruder.

There came unexpectedly a snatch of human voice. Though the cave's occupants could not have known its source, it came from the Priest.

"That hit on my head has scrambled my locaters."

The tentacle touched Fontaine's wetsuit, then Farrell's, and apparently having no interest in either, retreated back into the light from which it first came. And the light quickly vanished.

Ø

Given that much of an unexpected nature had already transpired inside the subterranean missile base, nothing less than the extremeness of the cold light and what it brought with it could have caused such a stir.

It had in all its iciness, materialized behind a rack in the radar-tracking chain.

The aspish tentacle had squirmed about into every corner of the complex and flicked its tongue at absolutely everyone in the room.

"There had leaked in with it another bit of distant conversation, this time Guinard's voice.

"Then I suggest you diagnose the malfunction and unscramble your precious locaters with unrestrained haste."

"Jeez Louise," wavered Magwood.

With a small clap then, like fresh thunder, the tentacle snapped back all along the twisted path it had taken through the complex. It slipped in reverse through the rupture that let it in. And it took the light with it.

Ø

The weaving beam of red light continued to dance to its own silent and internal rhythm as it twisted its way up and out of the open dome.

Its motion proved so nearly hypnotic that Padget and Cryer failed to spot the other light, the blue shivering one, until the moment the wormy tentacle wriggled out of its vortex and came toward them.

In spite of himself, Cryer let out a small shriek of alarm, which squeezed a similar sound from Padget.

"Unless you want me to saw open your head and repair the locaters myself."

The voice belonged to Guinard as he continued to berate the Priest, apparently still unaware of the open link.

And no doubt that icy voice, arriving as it had in perfect synchronicity with the segmented sensor's appearance on the scene played no small part in the two humans' mutual alarm.

"Run!" yelled Cryer.

"Where?!" demanded Padget.

Hers was a good question. The light and the probe had appeared between them and the dome's exit.

They ducked around the telescope base to avoid the thing; but it cornered Cryer and actually poked him experimentally in the center of his chest.

"Oh god!"

The tentacle jerked back, as if to something repellant in the contact. And it vanished at once in time with a muted crack of thunder.

Ø

There was a place out there, perfectly round, totally black, where not one star shone.

Kimama and Akando floated on the VentureStar's flight deck and peered out a side port hole.

They had both experienced a profound unease at their first experience with weightlessness. Akando had had to use a barf bag and suffer the indignity of hearing Kimama chide him about an earlier bean burrito.

Those initial problems had resolved themselves so quickly and completely that the two youthful Shoshones might almost have passed for old space hands, as floated and made continual awe-induced coos.

Alison Strong swam up behind them.

"Guess you figured that's the Earth," she said. "Usually, over here on the night side, there are bright rashes of lights, especially along the shorelines, cities and towns and such."

"No lights now," murmured Akando.

"No. Ah, but look."

They leaned forward to see where she pointed and saw just a thin arc of orange light starting to glide out over a sensuously curved horizon.

"First piece of daylight."

There was a small cough, like somebody clearing his throat. And a voice nearby whined, "I promise I'm doing my best."

"What?!"

Alison Strong did an acrobatic roll so that she faced where her back had been.

And where she looked was precisely the spot where the tentacle materialized.

It did so only inches from where Akando floated. And its appearance set him to thrashing about in the air, with no hand hold near enough to pull him away.

"I said, 'I'm doing my best'," the Priest's voice repeated.

Meantime, Akando had attacked the tentacle. He tried to bend it. Iye flew through upside down and joined the battle.

Akando looked at the others.

"You know, I could use a little help here!"

But the tentacle flung him off and turned toward Dan, then Kimama and Strong. It rudely stuck out its forked sensor and made a sort of raspberry sound. Then an instant later, it dematerialized.

Typically, it was Strong who offered the color commentary.

"Now if that don't give you cause to drop a few brownies, I sure as hell don't know what will."

Ø

The folk at the Sandy Cove Retirement Center never saw the light or the tentacle make its dramatic appearance.

It happened that way, because the spot of its materialization happened to be behind the trunk of a tall palm tree. And it was not until the segmented probing arm peeked around, like Satan from Eden's good-and-evil tree, that they were not even aware it was there.

When it had made its presence known to them, the Square Dancers and Misaka and Grigsby scattered like bugs from under a moved rock.

It was Guinard's voice that inflicted the greater fright.

"As usual, it seems that your best is not halfway good enough."

Misaka yelled, "Look out, Paul!"

Ø

To Fish, the freshly dug hole beneath the Machine in the Burwell's pasture smelled like the earth of a newly turned grave.

So profound was that feeling that he had, about forty-five minutes earlier, slumped into a bent-forward, positively fetal posture.

He had his back pressed hard against the most secure-looking part of the vertical wall.

He was humming to himself, a tune that might have been a comforting Yiddish lullaby recalled from his childhood.

Inches away, Zipper had engrossed himself in the process of removing one of the rings from his right ear.

So it was Fish who spotted the tentacle first and immediately stopped humming.

"Zipper."

"Uhm-huh."

"Uh … you might want to look at this."

Zipper looked up. "Oh, gods in hell!"

They both used their feet to scoot them on their butts away from the probe, which was making a thorough business of lashing all about in the tight space.

It slithered down the side of Fish's face, touching his cheek with its pointy tongue.

"No. No!"

He leaped up in a total panic and rammed his head against the Machine's bottom. Flesh and bone against alien composition was no fair contest. Poor Fish's knees buckled. He flopped flat. At the same time, the tentacle lost interest in him and turned toward Zipper.

The boy threw up a tattooed forearm, which the probe seemed to find particularly interesting.   It ran down the inked skin, starting at the elbow, and stopping just above the wrist on the oldest graphic, the clock face.

The disembodied voice said, "I have found him."

Another, quite familiar to the boy replied, "Bring him to me."

Just as Zipper yelled, "Get away!" the earring finally came loose in his hand and he threw it toward Fish's semi- conscious form.

"Catch!"

After that, it was only a game of fish-in-a-barrel. Zipper scrambled about the hole, ducked, rolled, all to avoid the tentacle's sweep and snatch.

And across the meadow, down the lane between the nester's tents, past the barn with Arabella and the new colt, through the kitchen window of the main house, they all heard Zipper's repeated screams.

Ø

Fish floated slowly back up from the blackness of unconsciousness into the blackness there in the hole beneath the Machine. And he found himself inexplicably alone.

As he rubbed a shiny, red spot on his forehead, he stupidly called out, "Zipper?!"

He heard movement approaching through the fallen leaves.

"Hey. I could use a little help over here!"

He listened. There definitely was a crunching sound. The steps grew closer.

"You're starting to freak me out I, —"

He turned just then and found two eyes, unblinking, yellow, peering in under the machine at him.

The wildcat snarled. Fish screamed.

The two of them dived off in opposite directions.

Chapter 13
"Rabbit Out Of A Hat"

The camouflage cloud banks were gone from the sky as seen through Sky Haven's gondola windows. The Atlantic Ocean undulated one way and the other near enough beneath the envelope to allow an occasional frothy splatter through the broken glass.

There was no longer any gunfire audible within the reception bay. There was, in fact, just a faint, mournful keening of the wind as it bent painfully in its passing around the great gas envelope.

But quite soon, there came on top of that pitiful wail, a distinctly human scream that seemed to coincide with the reappearance of the frigid light over near one of the windows.

That part of the room sparkled a bit as the light patch grew larger and turned about its center, some photonic Coriolis, in which its basic particles got themselves sucked straight down the rabbit hole and brought some desired thing along with it.

The scream started as a faint echo.

"Nooooooo!" cried the thing being dragged.

The panicky cry grew louder as the tentacle pulled its way up out of the whirl and his hiss inside the spiraling maw.

The transported object, coming feet first, turned out to be Zipper. And he brought his hysteria with him, its intensity growing all the worse, the instant his eyes settled on Guinard.

"Don't be afraid, my son," soothed Guinard as best his nature would allow. "The battle is all but over."

Zipper tried to run; but Guinard caught him.

"Stay with me or you will surely perish."

Chapter 14
"Ring Worm"

Fish massaged the lump on his head and examined his fingertips for blood. He seemed a little exasperated that there was none to be seen.

For at least the tenth time, he guided his eyes over the cramped space inside of the hole that he and the others had dug beneath the alien machine out in the Burwell's pasture land.

There was really not all that much to search. Any fool could see that he was totally alone. And yet, for what he knew was at least the third time he called out, "Zipper?"

Finally, he stood carefully and peeked out past the machine's low legs.

He could see in the distance the barn. But there appeared no one out there to rescue him from the hole.

He turned to look in a different direction and in doing so, his shoe sole pressed a shiny ring of a thing into the earthen floor.

Chapter 15
"All The Bodies?"

Guinard on one side and the Priest on the other compelled Zipper across one of the elevated walkways inside the amazing dirigible.

A noncom and two armed troopers waited for them at the far end. Guinard paused directly in front of the noncom.

"Where are Sepaca and Quigley?"

The noncom's eyes burned at the mention of those names.

"We chased Sepaca up toward the bow." He spit. "Quigley is everywhere. He's taken out a dozen of my best frontline troops."

Zipper had been looking around.

"Where are all the bodies?"

The noncom laughed and asked of Guinard, "He don't know?"

Without deigning to reply, Guinard yanked Zipper's arm; and, with the Priest on the other side as before, they headed off toward the front of the dirigible.

The noncom called after them, "You want we should escort you?"

Guinard ignored him.

Without so much as a hint of rancor, the noncom said to his troops, "Guess not."

They hesitated long enough to see Guinard, Zipper and the Priest fade into the gloom of defeat.

"That way," the noncom told his men; and they followed the walkway to where a small, dark corridor branched off to one side.

They seem prepared to walk on by, until a rather pronounced clank sounded from somewhere in its shadows.

The noncom signaled his troops; and they moved into the corridor.

Ø

Seeing as how it lay against the outside of the dirigible's airframe, the corridor turned out to be quite short.

The noncom and his two troopers moved into it with an obvious professional caution, within such a distance to provide quick assistance if needed, but spread out so as not to present a single, easy target.

They moved through occasional spots of dim light, around a gloomy lab entrance, on toward the end, and started to double back past a leafy greenhouse, wherein, unnoticed, one of the carnations abandoned its roots and slipped silently out behind the rear guard.

When the man chanced to look back, he found Quigley only inches away, one eye rolled back to show a hole from which a forked tendril shot out through his spectacle lens straight at the trooper's face.

It was the faint scrape of the eliminated man's shoe sole that turned one of the remaining troopers around.

"Sarge?"

The noncom looked back.

"Biggs was here a second ago."

The noncom's face said "panic".

"Let's get out of –"

His mouth stayed wide open, caught in a soundless scream, as a frosty light orbited his head and turned his flesh icy white.

And before the final trooper could save himself, a metallic whine cut the air and a shiny tentacle snared the man by his throat.

It was over in seconds, and the only betraying sounds were a few light dancing footsteps that the man's uncontrolled limbs made when he knew he was finished.

Quigley stood over the three, fastidiously straightened his tie. He removed his glasses, in which one of the lenses showed a small, neat hole through its center.

His eyes darted.

The air that touched his flesh was wrong. Someone else was sharing his space.

The corridor suddenly brightened to reveal Guinard, Zipper and the Priest blocking its only route out.

"I know you, Quigley," said Guinard through a tight smile. "I knew you could never resist them."

Chapter 16
"The Clay Man"

There in the corridor beside the flower stand, Quigley looked curiously at the Priest.

Guinard actually laughed.

"Well, after you deserted me, I needed someone to do my dirty work. And there were a few of your old parts lying around."

Zipper looked a Quigley, then watched as the three troopers' bodies quickly pull in on themselves and finally disappear into something not even there.

"You mean they aren't real?"

"All life is an illusion, Dear Boy."

And to Quigley Guinard said, "I suppose these were the last of my men."

The Priest leaned forward a bit over Guinard's shoulder. "Do you want me to take him?"

Briefly a bit of tentacle wiggled from his eye; and Quigley's eye responded in kind.

Guinard snorted.

"You? Made from his spare parts, with half the brain and spirit? I think not."

He reached into a side pocket on his coat and produced a fist-size ball of wire and sharp edges.

"Your master is not the only renaissance man Quigley. I whipped up this little something just in case we met up somewhere, sometime."

With that he freed the thing into the air, where it blossomed into a floating sphere with a dark, blinking heart.

For the first time, Quigley registered emotion. He drifted sideways, looking for a niche or a column that might give him some advantage of cover.

And Guinard said quite simply to the sphere, "Destroy the Clay Man."

"Clay Man," echoed Zipper.

And with the words still in Quigley's ear, the Sphere zipped through the air. Quigley evaded it, caught a wire frame with his tentacle and slingshot it back toward Guinard.

"Oh!" The Priest cowered.

Zipper ducked behind Guinard and watched the Sphere reverse itself sharply and head back at Quigley, traveling only inches off the floor.

The quarry was uncommonly fast, yet one of the sphere's cutters neatly sliced off one of Quigley's legs, which fell, bloodlessly, to the deck.

Quigley caught the sphere with one hand and hung on as it made another hard U-turn in the narrow corridor.

The device was truly a canny thing, planning to use the wall to its advantage.

The thing slammed Quigley into a wall. He came loose and landed hard.

Then the sphere went to the floor and rolled.

Quigley slid down the wall and landed directly in the thing's path. He crabbed to one side; but the Sphere was on him. It rolled one way, then another.

And soon Quigley lay diced and sliced and stacked into a pile of neat little sections, all bloodless, devoid of internal organs, as if made from a resilient form of putty.

They all stood a quiet watch for several moments, until finally Guinard turned to the Priest and said, "Get the watch."

The very idea clearly appalled the man. But his obvious fear of Guinard was greater; and, too, the razor ball was still rolling about spoiling for more action.

The Priest warily approached Quigley's remains, knelt and searched the shards of faux meat and clothing.

He looked up at Guinard.

"It isn't here."

Guinard waved his arm.

"Get away."

The Priest gladly made way for Ginard to stoop over the pieces and turn out what is left of the pockets, all which contained absolutely nothing.

Slowly he looked up, mouth set, eyes gone an actual red.

"Then Sepaca has it."

He pulled Zipper after him; and, after a final look at what had been Quigley, the Priest followed.

Chapter 17
"Rings A Bell"

F ish had both hands pressed over his eyes; and he was mumbling to himself.

"All right, I was a little dizzy from the hit on the head; but I was between Zipper and the tunnel. He could not have slid past me."

He pulled away his hands.

"And what's with that metal snake thingy? What was that supposed to be about?"

He leaned his back against the dirt wall and slid down to a seated position. He ran his gaze around the inside of the hole, letting his eyes come to rest on the floor near his toes, where something possibly metallic glittered up at him.

Slowly he leaned forward, not with any particular intention other than to determine the nature of the metal what's-it.

He dug at the thing with his fingernail.

It popped up, plopped down again, a few inches father away than before.

Definitely it was some sort of a metal ring. He reached out a bit more and plucked it up from the ground.

And as he absently cleaned the thing with his fingers, there came to his face an expression of distant recognition.

From off his butt, he rocked forward onto the balls of his feet, crouched directly beneath the Machine, and brought the ring up to the two empty holes in its bottom.

He pressed.

It snapped neatly, securely into place.

And immediately, the Machine went back to work. Inches from Fish's face, lines of alpha-numerics and symbols, familiar and obscure, danced in the air.

Row by row the columns fell shorter, until only one lonely zero remained.

Then the Machine beeped three times.

And it spoke to him, saying, "Warning: Quitting primary schedule. No restart option available."

"Yes!"

Fish almost jumped up, remembered his head and sat back on his haunches.

"It worked, by god, it worked!" And then in a much louder voice he said, "Somebody get me out of here!"

As if it arrived in distant answer to him, static briefly filled the hole, then cleared, as Padget's voice came through quite clearly.

"Just got a green light. We are good to go."

Chapter 18
"Star People"

Wind and water from the intensifying storm over Padre Island was in the process of rearranging the beach at the Species Language Center.

Airborne sand had already blasted most of the paint off the metal buildings still left standing. Roof and wall panels, some quite large, disengaged and flew knife-edged circles that sliced through a score of palm tree trunks that stood just inland.

There was a winking out there in the black water, a light. It rode a flotation ring up and down, ignoring the rip and swirl of the killer surf.

Farrell's voice came from somewhere.

"We're all set here."

A rush of water threatened to hurl the buoy onto the shore; but a thick black cable held it in place.

In fact the cable flexing up and down to accommodate the waves, led again to a cave entrance that opened only less than ten feet above the inlet's floor.

"Our translators are raring to go."

One of the dolphins said, "Hello, Star People."

"Not yet," Farrell told him.

Chapter 19
"All Together Now"

Hushed activity filled the abandoned missile base dug in a long ago political war beneath a remote piece of Colorado real estate.

Everyone moved on tip-toes.

Most conversation passed in mere whispers or, just as often, hand gestures or bad mime.

Over in one corner, given a wide berth by everyone but Shank, Odenwelder received and interpreted tracking information from off the facility's radar. Then, reformed into useful code, he fed the data into to their transmitter.

Shank grabbed a microphone.

"We're locked on the planetoid ... a very solid connection. You should be receiving our data stream just about now."

His words flashed half a continent away to the Sandy Cove Retirement Complex, where the Square Dancers worked furiously, continuously passing datum down the line to the seven team leaders, who fed it via their MindMeld caps straight into the bright bubbles all adrift over the surface of their cove.

Misaka grabbed her radio.

"We're on it. VentureStar, stand by for course correction data."

Somewhere a little more than three hundred miles above them, Alison Strong ordered Dan, Kimama and Akando to strap themselves in.

She keyed her mic.
"Just say the word; we'll fly this bird."
As if on cue, Kye landed on her head and the others laughed.
But all was not joy.

Chapter 20
"Bits And Pieces"

The injured dirigible creaked its pain, shuddered now and again as if trying to shake off its likely fate.

The once-bustling corridors stood vacant and silent of all human voice or cadenced footfalls.

The sunlight that slanted down through the translucent roof, lit the plants in a deserted flower stall, and slid across a jumble of bits lying near the terminus of a small, dead-end spur off the main concourse.

Quigley's pieces, heaped here, scattered there by Guinard's search for the pocket watch, lay across most of the companionway floor.

One section, unremarkable but for the closed eyelid in it, twitched just a little.

Maybe it was just some vibration coming up through the decking.

No.

Presently, the eye opened on its own. It looked around to the extent its circumstances would allow, then extended its tentacle.

Nearby, the other eye rose from its socket and watched as the tentacle began collecting the sundry parts and drawing them together through slices of Quigley's clothing.

The tentacle worked swiftly and with uncanny logic.

It first built limbs, then a torso and a head. And it stacked them in perfect anatomical order, until Quigley stood, where he had fallen, naked, well-muscled and, but for the lack of genitalia, looking quite human again.

He stretched and turned himself, perhaps to settle all the parts.

Then, with bare-footed pat, pat, pats, he set off at an Olympian's run.

Chapter 21
"Reading Zipper"

Three figures faced the deck-to-deck dull metal wall made of cleverly-joined panels.

Ator Guinard and the Priest gave every appearance of having arrived there under their own volition.

Zipper, by contrast, demonstrated his urgent preference for being elsewhere. He struggled constantly to escape Guinard's tight grasp.

There seemed little practical chance of that's happening, as Guinard held the boy firmly in check there before the hatchway.

Not that Guinard appeared entirely at rest himself. He fidgeted nervously as he watched the Priest pull a code generator away from the locking mechanism. The doorway would not open.

The Priest licked his lips nervously and turned to face his master.

"It's an orbiting code," he told Guinard in a frightened whisper. "It would take hours to puzzle it all out."

Guinard screeched, "Damn it all!"

He shoved Zipper off a few feet's distance from him and looked him over with more than a little reprehension.

And without the slightest trace of emotion, he said, "Remove your upper clothing."

The boy wrinkled his face in clear disgust.

"Not a chance."

Guinard's laugh burst over Zipper and the Priest as an explosion of rotted breath and rancid spittle.

They both seemed near to sickness.

"Do not honor yourself. I have no carnal interest in your putrid body. Nor do I have any such need of others, individually, in groups, human or bestial."

He extended the spur on his right hand.

The Priest whimpered reflexively and shrunk back.

"Now!" bellowed Guinard. "Expose your upper body, or I shall strip away the flesh and make use of it without its attachment to your worthless internal wriggles and twists!"

The Priest's knees buckled.

"Do it," he pleaded of Zipper. "Do it fast."

Zipper sensed the terror in the Priest's voice; and as quickly as possible, he shrugged out from inside the shirt and let the garment slide to the floor.

In the changing light, and with every small move of Zipper's meager musculature, the drawings seemed to move and mock in streams of colored ink that ran round and round him, up and down him, criss-crossed and spiraled, like some garish, animated stele.

"Scan him, Priest."

The Priest rolled back his eye and projected the cold light onto Zipper's skin.

"This won't hurt at all," he promised.

The glow slid over Zipper's chest and stomach and arms.

"Turn around, please."

Zipper seemed cold. He shivered, perhaps in the throes of terror. He turned so that his back faced the Priest and his eyes locked hatefully on Guinard.

And again the arctic light slid intimately down his back from the base of his hairline to his belt.

At that point, the glow finally shut off; and strangely, the Priest emitted a burp, as if he had just eaten a gourmand meal in obscene excess of all his wants or needs.

He closed his eyes.

"Feed me the data," ordered Guinard.

"I have done so," the Priest told him. "It is filed under 'ZipArt'."

Guinard's face grew slack for the briefest span, then assumed a jack-o-lantern facade that drew a shudder from the Priest and forced Zipper to wriggle with defensive haste back into the thin warmth of his shirt.

There followed the smallest interval in which nothing much seemed to happen.

But quite soon that changed, as even the dirigible resigned itself to Guinard's intimidation. The space inside the giant convex walls began to change their colors and adjust their shapes to a decidedly different will.

The great beast groaned and wheezed as its ribs popped and turned. The massive dorsal strut, Sky haven's spine, replaced and discarded vertebrae that fell in fist-sized chunks all around the three figures outside the bay door.

Through it all, Guinard's voice boomed like proximate thunder.

"I have beaten Sepaca. All he had is now mine. And soon, he will be mine as well, mind and heart!"

Even as the metamorphous continued on their every side, Guinard motioned to the Priest and intoned from a mask of heat and gloat, "Now give my Oracle the decoder."

And without pause for breathing, his mouth distended from the rest of his face and reached out toward Zipper, as he said, "And now you, worthless child, will open that door."

He shoved the Priest out of the way and roughly dragged Zipper up to within inches of the barrier.

But, lower lip atremble, Zipper slowly shook his head.

"I will not help you open it."

Guinard made a soft purring sound, a sweet contrast to what was about to come. He snuggled menacingly close to Zipper and stroked his hair. And in a voice made of ragged steel, he said into Zipper's ear, "Do not test me, child. For I do not have time for this."

His teeth clacked, clinched and unclenched.

"There will be others here soon and we must be gone by then."

Then he yanked the generator from the Priest's hands and pressed it hard against Zipper's chest.

"I believe one of your new friends is a charmingly innocent girl named Sara."

Zipper's eyes bounced nervously in their sockets.

Yet again, Guinard raised his hand and extended the razor-sharp spur, a move that caused the Priest to flinch with personal dread.

"Or would you like me to bring her here, as I have brought you, so that you can watch me strip the flesh from her body?"

Zipper's mouth worked, as if suppressing a gag. Still he hesitated.

"You and I together can listen to her scream as she slowly dies."

"Okay," Zipper whispered. "Please, please don't."

He took the generator from Guinard's hands, made only a very few adjustments and pressed it to the lock.

Immediately soft churnings arose from deep inside the door. It clanked, its parts stirred, separated, and slid fully apart from one another.

Chapter 22
"I'll Take The Watch"

At first only a little light fell into the forward cargo bay through the doors, which were still disengaging their complex individual sections from one another and sliding slowly apart.

What illumination did leak in from the corridor outside served to push three long shadows over the threshold, past rows of tied-down containers that filled most of the huge and murky space.

There were, all around, hints of many connected levels that all ended in a blunt, convex curve at the farthest end.

Guinard and the Priest came in on their own. Zipper needed mostly to be dragged by Guinard.

They stopped a few feet inside. The alien tilted his horned head and listened to the huge space.

The smack of his lips came from deep within the shadows across his face.

He said quite loudly, "I hear your heartbeat, Sepaca, louder than my own."

"I don't hear anything," announced Zipper querulously.

Guinard advanced a few more steps, hauling Zipper along beside him.

The Priest followed on his own.

There was definitely a sound then.

Zipper heard it, too, looked toward the high skeletal ribs, where everything bowed inward at the very tip of the dirigible's snout.

Something moved there, an umbra slithering over the steel ribs.

The Priest spotted it, too.

"There!"

"I see it," Guinard sneered. And then louder, he called out, "It's the finish line, Sepaca."

The shadow stepped finally out onto one of the lower spars and, extending his arms for balance, rode it, standing, all the way to the floor, coming to a stop no more than twenty feet from Guinard.

The two of them, Sepaca and Guinard, appraised one another for several dead-silent seconds, each as if he had never seen anything so strange as the other.

Finally Guinard was the only one who had anything he needed to say.

"I'll take the watch now."

Sepaca looked surprised.

"You didn't find it then?"

There was a deep-level growl to the bay, something like a barely-controlled savagery that eventually formed an underlay to Guinard's voice, as he said, "The game is over, Sepaca. I have a planet to conquer. Give me the watch. Now."

"Sorry, I really do not have it."

Just then, a fresh shadow, drifting along bare foot soles, came in to join them.

"Monsieur Guinard," called out Quigley.

Guinard, Zipper and the Priest turned in time to see Quigley open his mouth and push out the watch with his tongue.

Guinard yelled, "No!"

He shoved the Priest. "Stop him!"

But before the Priest could move, Quigley raised his left arm up into the air and began swinging the watch at the end of its fully-extended chain, round and round above Quigley's head.

Guinard's eyes widened, followed the watch in flight. It went around again and once more.

Then, carefully guided by Quigley, the thing made one more orbit, dipped and then smashed edgewise, hard against the nearest bulkhead.

The crash it made was like the colliding of two speeding freight trains.

It shattered, the watch did, into hundreds of parts that flew outward from the point of collision and rained all over the storage bay.

Then Quigley threw himself at Guinard and the Priest and wrapped his arms hard around them.

As they fought, there appeared suddenly an even dozen razor straight slashes of light, like primal leaks through the cosmic weave, materializing along twelve different tracks, each path passing through parts of the tumbling watch parts, until they were all connected.

Guinard wailed, "Release me, Clay Man. I command it!"

But the words garbled in his throat as the grand airship began to fold inward on a single blaze of white-hot energy centered on the crumbling gold watch case bouncing, bouncing across the floor.

Zipper screamed and hugged himself as if to keep from being torn apart. Sepaca captured the boy in his own arms and dragged him toward a tear that hung in the air like a rapidly-closing doorway.

"Hurry!" gargled Sepaca's voice.

They went through just as the breach closed and sealed the fates of all who remained.

Ø

Three distinctly new sources of consciousness entered the very old place, more ancient by far than Earth, more ancient than the Milky Way galaxy, and far older than much of the known human universe.

Amongst those three new arrivals, there was but one soul.

There existed nothing organic about him. He had been, in fact, in all physical ways, an artificial life form.

But he had been more humane than most others, real or handmade, ever to make the transition through The Wall.

He drifted free of agony.

The other two knew immediate torture.

Yet they occupied the same space.

The first thing they noticed about such an old collection point was that there already existed therein a great and horrible lamentation, like all of Earth's inhabitants in the millions of years of evolution across its surface had, at one agreed-upon time, assembled to cry out their disappointments and harmful acts and lack of faith in something, anything.

Those billions of voices joined in an eerie harmonic.

And in that distorted reality, Guinard's body and the Priest's stretched and bent as if drawn down hard upon a surrealistic canvas.

How then to explain Quigley?

He occupied the same place as the others.

Yet he lamented nothing, felt no pain, retained his perfect, artificial shape.

The same vortex caught them, had drawn them through the horizon, snapped some dimensional string, sucked all three down a cosmic drain, and from there on to a sphere of black and gray filled with a mingling of tortured and rapturous shapes.

The loudest were those of the tribulation.

Marching boot soles slapped hard pavement.

Voices grew hysterical in their united shouting.

"Sieg heil! Sieg heil! Sieg heil!"

Burning wood crackled somewhere.

A woman screamed and cried in French, "God please help me, I'm not a witch!"

A growling, angry mob grumbled, "Hang the nigger!"

Only one amongst them all might yet be saved.

Chapter 23
"Stepping Back"

That same place, at a reasonable remove, revealed energy wisps, self-illuminated from their own internal furnaces, all at a swirl about a gaping black pit through space.

The hole itself floated within a blazing halo of large and small stars, all at war with the gravity well, swimming with all their might just to keep from falling in.

The Milky Way's fat, dense center twisted dizzily about its violent heart.

From such vast distances, all of the galaxies looked unbearably beautiful and all perfectly at peace with themselves, their pinwheel arms arced out to embrace the blackest of space.

Eventually, in all the parsecs between the last light in the final twisted arm and the next nearest star, all dimmed to a cold, cold nothingness, where only the bravest of panspermia ever set sail.

The occasional lonely and unlighted planet drifted by, the largest amongst them, perhaps, sufficiently heated by internal tectonics to support a barest snippet of life.

Such was the course of things out where only raw organic things made their stealthy way unseen.

Chapter 24
"What The Cat Drug In"

On the Burwell farm, the day had dawned uncommonly bright and disposed of promising things yet to come.

The urban squatters, welcomed by the Burwell family onto their land during the previous several days of total technological collapse, had seen the glow of the nearest city reappear in the middle of the night just past. In preparation for departure and, presumably, a resumption of their former lives, they were all in some stage of packing up whatever they had brought with them, the bits that still held some value for the future.

A few amongst them thought to gather the refuse of their stay, bag it and, in some cases, that of their immediate neighbors, and stack it for disposal.

Fewer still made a point of expressing their gratitude to Seth Burwell of his having offered them a decent place of refuge.

In most spots, paper blew, apple cores and orange peels browned and rotted, and the makeshift tents sagged and collapsed in abject abandonment.

Out in the meadow, close by the Machine, Fish and the Burwell family survey the mess without much display of emotion.

Seth said, "I know it doesn't sound all that Christian. But for all the trouble they brought, I'm plenty happy to see them gone."

Fish seemed not to be listening.

"I should have known it was him all along."

"Who?" asked Seth.

"Zipper. From the first time I laid eyes on him, I had a feeling in my bones that he was a bad apple that would make it all go wrong."

Sara shook her head with obvious sadness.

"I just can't believe it. He seemed so real. There must have been some reasons we don't know about."

Seth thought, "Maybe not all of the choices were his to make. And you said he did leave you the thing you needed to shut down the machine."

Fish opened his mouth as if to add or subtract the odd thought, and held his words in response to a peculiar jingling sound way up in the trees.

"That's strange," said Seth.

Stranger still the manner in which the proximate world about them abruptly rippled so forcefully that it staggered all four of them, nearly to a fall.

Miriam looked around wide-eyed.

"What was that?"

Sara pointed excitedly.

"Zipper!"

They all followed her gaze and saw Zipper stumble and fall to his knees, try to stand, and drop again onto all fours.

In a fury, Fish rushed at him and yanked him up by his shirt front.

"You rotten, worthless little bastard!"

He drew back his fist with the clear intent of punching Zipper full in the face.

But Seth caught and held back the cocked arm.

"Mister Fishbourn. Please. No violence."

Still, Fish shook Zipper rather forcefully.

"You're got a real set coming back here after what you did."

Zipper moved his lips, but no words would come out yet"

So Fish filled the silence with his own rage.

"Well someday, our paths will cross again, you can be sure of that, Zipper, if that's your real name."

Zipper staggered, nearly fell again.

For some reason, Fish felt compelled to hold him up.

And when Zipper finally was able to speak, his voice sounded as if it were somewhere else, and possibly had not yet caught up with his body.

"Don't blame you," he rasped.

He shook his head to clear the fuzz.

"And just so you'll know – maybe so you'll have another reason to hate me – my real name is Zerbino Guinard."

Fish's jaw dropped.

"Guinard? Your father?"

"I was eight. Already good with computers. He adopted – no, not really – he bought me out of an orphanage up in Quebec."

He looked sad-eyed at Sara.

"As for why I came back."

Chapter 25
"Finally Some Answers"

A bit over three hundred miles straight up from the Burwell farm, the flight deck on the VentureStar's resonated with a sharp, whip-like crack, and suddenly, as if surfacing from a watery soak, Sepaca appeared. He, seemingly a bit confused, as he floating in the air amongst Dan, Kimama and Akando.

Strong looked around from the command seat.

"Well, guys," she said, "looks like we might finally be about to get us some answers."

The appearance that Sepaca might have appeared amongst them in a dazed condition quickly passed.

He said out loud, perhaps as much to himself as to the others, "I really do hate doing that."

As to the effect Sepaca's sudden appearance had made on the ship's crew, only Alison Strong was unimpressed.

"Where to, Mister Sepaca?" she wondered with a sly smile that said she already knew the answer.

Sepaca kicked off toward one of the crew couches, swung himself into the harness and said, "Let's go see our friends."

The others drifted quickly to their own seats and strapped themselves in.

Chapter 26
"Space Place"

A snow-blinding light reflected off most of the spheroid's shiny surface and painted long, rotating shadows on the sheltered side of instrument bays, antennae, struts, panels and such like.

With excruciating slowness, a spot of white rising from the murky Earth's atmosphere grew steadily larger and more clearly defined.

Thin delta wings soon revealed themselves, as did a tall stabilizer fin and a motor assembly.

The VentureStar made a cautious lover's approach, puffing passionate kiss-like adjustments from vents all along its shiny skin.

A rectangle of light opened itself invitingly near the planetoid's equator.

Almost timidly the spacecraft slipped nearer and finally made entry through the docking port, which sealed itself securely behind it.

Chapter 27
"Listen To The Dolphins"

The VentureStar settled with impressive precision onto a flashing platform near the center of a vaulted chamber which, itself, lay separated from the rest of the planetoid's interior by a wide, clear wall.

The spaceship's crew all undid their seat harnesses and stood up, the better to reacquaint their legs with the return of one-G gravity.

Like the others, Sepaca climbed out of his couch. But as the outer hatch began slowly to open, he tarried near the rear of the pack and motioned them along ahead of him.

Akando wondered if he could take Iye in with him.

"It would be only fair," Sepaca told him. "The journey has been his as much as yours or the other humans on all the other teams."

Akando smiled.

"Of course, we would not be here without their help."

"You would do well to remember that," said Sepaca as they passed him on their way outside. "As the memories of these times start to dim, make sure you continue to credit the horses and the dolphins and even the coral reef."

Dan seemed to be the first to realize that Sepaca was intentionally lingering just inside the hatchway.

"You're not going?"

"Just this far."

He gestured for Dan to step on through. Alison Strong stopped beside him.

"That first day, sitting around the conference table, at your house, it crossed my mind this might turn out to be some kind of a test."

"A test?" echoed Kimama.

Akando asked if such a test would be designed to measure their courage.

Strong said, "My own guess, personally, is that it all was about our capacity for cooperation with one another."

Sepaca nodded.

"Imagine how completely all of you would have failed had even one taken a single, selfish step."

Strong and Kimama stepped out onto the ramp.

Dan looked out after her and paused, apparently uncertain. He turned back to face Sepaca.

"Will they speak English?"

Sepaca laughed with genuine delight.

"Just listen to the dolphins, Dan."

Akando stepped out with Iye riding on his shoulder.

Dan was the last to go through.

Chapter 28
"Inside"

The docking bay in which they had come to rest was a marvel. But it amounted to nothing at all compared to what the crew beheld when they came down the ship's ramp and gazed out through the tall, transparent shield.

There lay a miraculous world out there, wherein waterfalls poured from voids at its core onto a surface that constantly rose, so that by looking straight up, one viewed the emerald tops of trees and building roofs on the opposing hemisphere.

"Oh my word," wheezed Dan.

Alison Strong snorted.

"Kinda makes you feel like some kind of a damned ant, don't it?"

Ø

To everyone's surprise, it was cautious Akando, giving Iye a ride on his shoulder, who regained his composure first and led the way down the ramp.

Dan, Alison Strong and Kimama watched him approach the transparency; and in amazement, they saw four humanoids of sundry size and body mass advancing to greet him.

Akando raised one weaponless hand.

The aliens responded in kind.

"Well, he's not having all the fun," said Kimama.

She descended after him and Dan and Alison followed.

Just as they reached the bottom of the ramp, a portal opened in the transparency; and their came out the most delightful sounds.

There was music, like a mix of children laughing and rain drops falling through a forest canopy.

It drifted around the two parties, embraced them and almost physically drew them into a single collective there on the threshold.

The tallest alien, who stood well over seven feet and strikingly resembled Sepaca, touched each human on the forehead and said something almost recognizable.

It went, "Fel gon. Too hag maht brate chur may ed beggy vaz."

And there came almost immediately a sweet piping out of Dan's radio, one of the dolphins translating, "Him say, 'You welcome. Make a great journey in many ways'."

Dan half bowed.

"We're glad to finally meet you."

The Tall Alien said, "Too ab prit ahn fahn tee."

And the dolphin echoed, "Him say, 'You split a infinitive.'"

A human voice, Frank's, slipped into a brief silence on the radio.

"Dan, this is Frank Farrell speaking from Camp David. I'm here with President Beaton and some of his advisors."

"Mister President," Dan replied with no evident enthusiasm.

The president's voice came again out of the small speaker.

"Hello, Dan. With you as a go-between, we'd like to try and hammer out some kind of an agreement that'll get us back on the road to a full recovery for the billions of human beings down here on Earth."

"The Tall Alien replied, "Ooie aht bol tee canz."

Down on the Earth's surface, beneath the surface, in fact, Farrell and Fontaine continued to paddle nearby as the Dolphins chattered through their foreheads into the suction cup receptors.

Dolphin Two translated the Tall Alien's last comment.

"Him say, 'Phooey on politicians'."

Dan's voice came out of Farrell's radio.

"Our team is at your service, Mister President."

And President Beaton's voice came through again, saying, "Good. Now what is it exactly they want from us?"

Chapter 29
"Trading Places"

Zipper came to the top of the staircase and paused. He had, draped over one arm, a large cloth sheet made up of dozens of smaller colorful material scraps.

He paused there and listened to the sound of a woman's voice singing. He imagined it was probably Sara's, pure and beautiful, floating up to sooth his wounded soul.

What was it she sang? The tune struck familiar chords; but the words were foreign.

That was it. The language was not English. It was some sort of German, but not any with which he was familiar, and German was one of his better alternate tongues.

Oh, but that melody.

What? She had stopped singing.

He sighed and walked the twenty feet that took him down the hallway to Caleb's room, where the door stood open.

Caleb was stuffing personal items, clothing, a small radio with yellow earphones, into a small canvas bag.

Zipper stepped into the doorway.

"Your father said I can stay for a while, at least till I make up my mind about what to do next."

Caleb turned, saw the folds of fabric over Zipper's arm and smiled. "Ma makes quilts for people she likes."

"Sara helped her."

Caleb returned to his packing, "Sara's not like me. She's truly rooted here. She won't ever go away with you."

Zipper shrugged and mumbled, "I feel like maybe I could make up for some of the wrong-headed things I've done."

Caleb grinned.

"By my understanding, you've already done that. A real folk legend, huh?"

Zipper seemed genuinely embarrassed by the thought.

"Afraid I don't have any sense of that."

Caleb glanced up now and again from his labors and finally said, "I give you a week before they cart you off to the loony bin."

He closed the bag and they left the room together, walked silently into the hallway and started down the stairs.

"New York is it?" asked Zipper.

Caleb nodded.

"I spent most of the night working on a musical about what all's happened."

As they approach the bottom of the stairs, Caleb said, "It's called 'Dancing In The Dark'."

Zipper laughed, genuinely delighted. "All right. I like it."

Ø

Fish stood just outside the white washed picket fence in front of the Burwell house. He was making a conscious business of admiring the roses that Miriam Burwell liked to say, "Are a first greeting to whomever comes to visit our home."

She was up on the porch with Seth and a couple of Amish men. They were all paying uncommon attention to an anachronism right there in their very own yard. It had the form of a rather nice looking automobile.

Very soon, Caleb and Zipper appeared through the front door; and the men, getting their first good look at Zipper, could not help but raise their eyebrows, ever so slightly.

Seth chided them confidentially, "Give him a chance, why don't you?"

Fish came back through the gate and looked at Caleb's only bag.

"That's all of your luggage?"

Caleb nodded.

"I intend to maintain a simple life style, Mister Fish. No point in losing my head."

"Absolutely. I'll put that in the car for you, while you say your goodbyes."

"Just a few seconds," Caleb told him.

"Take as long as you need."

As Fish took the bag to the car, Caleb turned to Miriam. Tears weld in her eyes as she embraced Caleb and kissed his cheek.

He bussed her forehead. "I'll write. Promise."

Sara's lower lip was trembling.

"We've been together all our lives," she quavered. "I'll have lost my other half."

He kissed her cheek, too, and straightened a wayward tress of her hair.

By the time he turned to Seth, he seemed to have run out of words.

So it was Seth who spoke.

"We're always here, if ever there's a need, son."

Caleb heaved a great breath that rattled with angst.

"Thanks, Pa."

He stopped just short of the first step, turned and wrapped his arms around his father's neck.

"You've always been my hero," he said. "Always will be."

Then, without another word, he went down the steps. He and Fish climbed into the car and they drove away over the familiar ruts of the dirt road that led out to the interstate.

They were observed through a twist of berry vines. The tufted-eared wildcat watched them pass. He shook his head as if to lose the collar with its flashing light. But it would not budge.

Chapter 30
"Facing The Cameras"

The Potomac River, despite its unceasing motion, looked rested and refreshed beneath a sunny mid-morning sky.

The nation had awakened to the return of electric power and the steady, mostly inane flow of electronic information.

On this particular day, however, there were things more important than the latest celebrity improprieties.

By then, everyone knew that sentient beings from far away stars had come visiting. They had briefly, but frighteningly, robbed Earth's inhabitants of all that gladdened their collective hearts.

And though most folk had not the slightest idea or – for that mater – interest in how it had happened, the problem had been corrected in time for the day's entertainment oriented news shows.

Everyone knew the weather in Washington, D.C., earlier threatened with the possibility of rain, would be clear and sunny over the Capitol Building by the time representatives of the nation's leadership assembled themselves on the southern steps.

But even forewarned, the media crews were still in a scramble, when Frank, Dan, Fish and Tiffany came down to face the microphones and cameras.

Naturally, the Senate Majority Leader and House Speaker had position themselves so as to form a prominent backdrop for the news conference.

Frank waited a few seconds for everything to settle down, then he looked up at the cameras.

"The President has asked me to thank you for the way most of you behaved during our just-ended crisis. And he has instructed me to relay to you some of the details contained in an agreement he and other leaders have reached with a delegation from the Orion Alliance."

A reporter in the front ranks called out, "That's what the aliens call themselves?"

"That is correct. They represent more than two hundred separate worlds."

A second reported asked, "Does that mean we've thrown up our hands and surrendered? Are you saying no military response is being planned?"

Frank pulled a slightly hostile face and snapped, "You see, your asking that question shows why the off-worlders are afraid of us."

"Does that mean the answer to my question is that there will be no military response?"

Frank looked away from the reporters and directed his response directly through the cameras to the viewing audience around the world.

"There definitely will not be any military action from us in response to what has happened over the past two days."

A third reporter piped up.

"As long as you're talking for the President, would you care to tell the American people why their government has consistently lied to them about UFOs for fifty years?"

Frank nodded.

"That's a fair question, George. But I think this might be exactly the wrong time to search out an appropriate answer. The truth is that if we look back now instead of directing our vision forward, we're gonna stumble; and we cannot afford to miss this chance."

At that same time, some of the eyes and ears tuned in to the broadcast belonged to folk directly involved in the unseen drama that had filled the previous two days.

Inside an observatory dome atop a ridge in southern New Mexico, a radio played a backdrop as Louise Padget and Hollis Cryer peered skyward through the reflecting telescope. Their field of vision was mostly filled by a view of the alien planetoid as it tracked slowly behind the moon's dark edge

Frank was saying, "The first step in the agreement took place earlier this morning, when the Alliance raised its base into an orbit just beyond Earth's natural satellite, our ancient, sometimes deified companion in the cosmos."

There were, to be sure, views inside the artificial world that day.

Kimama, Akando, with eyes still aglow at all the wonders around them, stood with Iye, who was, himself, a marvel to the dozens of Aliens of various descriptions watching a giant, open-air screen located in a perfectly-manicured park.

They all seemed to understand what Frank was saying from far below on the Capitol Steps.

"In the second phase, they have already begun restoring complete use of our technology, a factor, of course, which makes this broadcast and your viewing of it possible."

The hushed crowd of humanity gathered about the Capitol's façade had grown quite somber by the time Frank looked out at the circle of cameras.

"The third phase is completely up to us. The Alliance has given the people of Earth ten years to get our house in order. If we do a halfway decent job of it, there's a good chance they will invite us to join their union."

A reporter's voice came from the throng.

"And if we're not suitably house broken by then?"

All the way down in southern Texas, as Alvin Farrell and Ursula Fontaine picked through the wreckage made of their Inter-Species Language Center by the hurricane, they listened to Frank on a portable radio.

"From the way I've heard it described, it would be something like a zoo, I think."

The two dolphins swimming off shore seemed to be listening, too.

"Using their technology, the Alliance would establish a sort of a containment field around the Earth; and we would be caged here forever."

Farrell and Fontaine stopped where they were, beside a crushed building. An eerie silence came to them through the radio.

Finally Frank added, "I agree. It isn't very appealing."

At the Sandy Cove Retirement Complex, Natalie Misaka and Paul Grigsby watched a TV, while the residents square danced, with the Coral Computer doing the calling.

"There's something else," Frank told them from the TV. "The President has ordered the breakup of the international monopoly ACRONYM into smaller units, which I can already hear you calling "Baby Ubies"."

A couple of the Square Dancers came after Misaka and Grigsby and pulled them into the fun.

The coral computer provided the calls, "Swing your partners; watch your feet; you're dancing on a coral reef."

On the television screen, Frank brought in two familiar faces to join him at the mics.

"To implement the actual dissolution, I have called on these two gentlemen, Dan Diamond and Philo Fishbourn."

The cameras focused on Dan and Fish.

And the coral computer finished its call, "We sea creatures down below, wish that we could doe-see-doe."

Back on the Capitol Building steps, Frank glanced over at Tiffany and they smiled at one another.

"One final announcement," said Frank. This one is of a purely personal nature. One of the nation's most respected media figures, Miss Tiffany Diamond, whom you see on my left, has agreed to become my partner in marriage, the exact date to be decided after things settle down a little bit."

The crowd offered a smatter of polite applause.

Not far away in miles, on the site of Neil Sepaca's cultural center, only a few yards from the wreckage of his former mansion residence and headquarters, there stood an enormous building, so recently added to the location that it might well have gone up overnight.

Inside its great open space, sparks flew from an army of welders at work on an enormous, streamlined framework.

Two men in hard hats watched a small TV set on a large table otherwise covered with sheets and rolls of complex blueprints.

Frank's image played on the television screen.

"Miss Diamond and I can tell you that, when it is finished, we will be married aboard Mister Neil Sepaca's new airship, the Sky Haven II."

Inside the construction hanger, one of the men at the blueprint table offered a rare smile.

As he turned from the TV, Neil Sepaca looked out over the metal skeleton of his new airship and he seemed as contented as any of his species was able.

Chapter 31
"Old Games Die Hard"

Straight-trunked conifers encircled the collection of rustic frame buildings, which at the moment seemed deserted.

The same was true of the watchtowers that stood at all four of the corners of a twelve-foot high fence of razor wire and high-voltage lines.

A voice from some unseen source intruded into the unlikely setting.

"Congressman Farrell, has General Sahura of the Western Nile Republic and other rogue leaders accepted this union?"

Inside the complex, there is slight movement near the corner of one of the buildings.

Joel Shank slipped cautiously into view. He was wearing goggles and fatigue clothing. And he carried a wide-barrel rifle.

On the hidden radio, Frank responded to the question.

"I assume you're speaking of my pending marriage to Miss. Diamond?"

A little laughter seeped into the compound.

Shank squatted and surveyed the buildings and the trees. Then he made a hand signal; and several Militiamen slipped from hiding and followed him toward a second structure some forty feet away.

The soft crunch of their boot soles was muffled by a carpet of pine needles and further camouflaged by the ongoing radio broadcast.

Frank could be heard saying, "Seriously, my hope is that after today, the General Sahuras of the world will only be found in museums, along with land mines and laser-guided bombs such tyrants often employ against their own people."

Shank's unit had covered only a few yards, when dozens of paintball packets rocketed from numerous places of cover.

One of Shank's men took a hit that left him bathed in a bright yellow ooze.

Frank was saying, "But human nature rule number one holds that the guys at the top are always the last to buy into anything that limits their power."

From the opposite side of the compound, Odenwelder leaped suddenly upright and led his men from behind a stack of railroad ties and straight at Shank. Paint flew in every direction. Shank's men fell back.

Another question from yet another reporter came out of the radio.

"If that's rule number one, Congressman, I'm just wondering, is there a rule number two?"

And just as Odenwelder's force seemed to gain the upper hand, Magwood's unit swept in from behind, pelting their opponents as they came.

Soon men, rocks, trees, buildings, all bore yellow stains.

Frank could be heard saying, "Yes. Rule number two holds that primal changes never come from the few. They take root in the hopes and dreams of the many."

Chapter 32
"Eat Cake"

Rivers of humanity coursed out of the narrow, cobbled streets of historic old Paris. They surged into the Rue de Rivoli on the Right Bank and came up out of the Latin Quarter along Boulevard Du Saint Michel on the Left Bank.

Inside one of the great vintage buildings filled with tiny flats along the way, someone had tuned in the broadcast from Washington, D.C.; and they had cranked the volume up loud so that Frank's voice spilled out over one of the balconies.

"And from the many, those primal changes inevitably boil their way upward and eventually consume the undeserving princes of pride and privilege."

Shouting people emptied the apartment buildings and office structures and joined the advancing throng.

It seemed without their being told or having arrived at any sort of consensus, they all knew where they were heading.

Other swelling legions merged on the Champs Elysees north of the Arc De Triomphe and, also set a course toward the Seine.

All along the quais that bounded the river's banks they squeezed their ranks in the direction of Pont-Neuf and Pont Saint-Louis.

Their momentum carried them onto the bridges. And with their bodies they smashed through the barricades that blocked the ways onto the Ile de La Cite.

The guards outside the cathedral did their terrified best to stem the flow; but they were soon driven over the balustrades and into the water.

Once through the outer fortifications, the mob rushed round the cathedral from every direction, abusing the guards in their flight.

Within minutes, the ACRONYM sign crashed down from the glorious front entrance of the cathedral.

The scene continued thus, with small fires here and there, from the early afternoon until well after dawn the following day.

And by the time the sun had fully risen, the People had made sure that there was not even one visible sign of ACRONYM anywhere in all their recaptured city.

Chapter 33
"Original Sin"

The joy came palpably through the floors and walls of the Notre Dame Cathedral, even shook a little dust from the supports down upon the masses gathered below.

Colored sunlight poured through the great Rose Window and painted a procession of robed men and boys following a tall golden cross and a phalanx of smoking incense burners.

Organ notes carried the worshipers' souls aloft.

An enormous choir sang with unexcelled thanksgiving, an anthem that was both sacred and a powerful.

And as the faithful knelt for prayer, there was in one window depicting a stained glass Garden of Eden, a scene in which the Serpent offered Eve the apple.

Chillingly, the Serpent had a most familiar countenance. It was unmistakably the face of Ator Guinard.

And as the procession passed slowly by, the snake's image curled about the Tree of Knowledge and the reptilian eyes followed the uplifted crucifix.

And the bishop's voice floated out over the throng as he said, "Let us give thanks to God in prayer for our deliverance."

Half a world away, church bells rang from an old white wooden steeple.

Goggles reached down and grasped Tiffany's gloved fingers in his own.

Frank made a saddle of his hands for the toe of her satin shoe; and together, they swept her smoothly up into the basket that hung beneath the balloon's inflated envelope.

The three of them waved to an assembly of onlookers, which included President Beaton and Tiffany and Frank's fathers.

Everyone cheered and waved back, as Goggles opened the fuel valve to increase the upward flow of heated air.

Ground crews cast off the lines.

The basket swayed a bit as it departed its moorings and rose ever so slowly, elegantly toward the bluest sky most of them agreed they had ever seen.

Ricky Escobar, his camera balanced on one shoulder, had the zoom lens trained on them at just the instant when someone released a flock of at least two dozen white doves that followed the balloon in its ascent, with some of the birds circling round and round the archaic craft as the proper wind direction caught it and guided it away toward the southwest.

With the whoosh of the burner and the passing of the wind, the bells faded quickly into the distance.

... epilogue

The pitch-black nothingness hummed a perfect G-flat. Time surrendered all relevance, but for the glitter and twist of gears and springs.

Where a crystal tumbled, wheels turned without connecting cogs.

A tiny key having nothing to wind, twisted with the rest of it all at the end of its gold chain and fluttered in no discernable direction.

Two graceful human hands, opposable thumbs, reached; one folded round some few of the time parts; the other grasped the rest.

"Give me the pieces you've caught, Quigley, and I will share the power with you."

"Return to me the pieces you have stolen, Ator, and I will not destroy the ones that I have found."

Solitary laughter mingled like water with the oily wailings of despair.

THE ROSWELL CHRONICLES
The Next Chapter:
"Trial Run"

...now

"You do remember agreeing to host the para-plant, don't you?" asked the alien who fizzed before Kimama Sweet's eyes like a pale and lazy cyclone. "The others have all consented."

The thought passed quickly through Kimama's mind that each of the countless "snowflakes" in the being's tight vortex contained a single bacterium.

They had confided that much to her earlier. And she seemed to recall how it was the light show up and down the core of the dancing cloud that carried the cognitive transmissions that tied all those microscopic corpora into a whole and highly intelligent being.

"Your question uneases me," Kimama said-thought toward the whirl and twist of it. "It sounds like one last chance to back out of something I might later regret."

"It will tie you to the others. When the sleep comes, you will know of its approach with ample time to find a place of refuge. And you will dream together even as you see us doing now."

"Tell me again why this is a good thing."

...then

The alien spun back from Kimama a bit, lifted itself a foot or two off the deck, and whispered, "You will do the best of all good things."

Lightning flashed up and down its spine.

"You and the others will accomplish nothing less than the ultimate salvation of humanity."

"Yes, I remember now."

"And you are ready?"

Kimama licked her lips.

"I am."

"Well then ..."

The spout circled her once, as if searching for something in particular. Then a long, thin line of its internal fire struck out through the gap between them and entered Kimama's left temple.

Suddenly she was afloat in a profusion of green leaves and branches full of bird songs and an atmosphere steaming with earthy smells.

Somewhere nearby, a jaguar screeched.

Kimama realized she was already dreaming.

...infinity